MITCHELL'S RUN

MITCHELL'S RUN

Amy Gallow

CHIVERS
THORNDIKE

This Large Print book is published by BBC Audiobooks Ltd, Bath, England and by Thorndike Press®, Waterville, Maine, USA.

Published in 2005 in the U.K. by arrangement with Saltwater Press.

Published in 2005 in the U.S. by arrangement with Dorian Literary Agency.

U.K. Hardcover ISBN 1–4056–3427–8 (Chivers Large Print)
U.S. Softcover   ISBN 0–7862–7849–8 (Buckinghams)

The text of this Large Print edition is unabridged.
Other aspects of the book may vary from the original edition.

Set in 16 pt. New Times Roman.

Printed in Great Britain on acid-free paper.

British Library Cataloguing in Publication Data available

Library of Congress Cataloging-in-Publication Data

Gallow, Amy.
     Mitchell's run / by Amy Gallow.
          p.   cm.
     "Thorndike Press large print Buckinghams"—T.p. verso.
     ISBN 0–7862–7849–8 (lg. print : sc : alk. paper)
     1. Australia—Fiction. 2. Large type books. I. Title.
PR9619.4.G35M58 2005
823'.92—dc22   2005012126

MITCHELL'S RUN

1

'If you are a typical example, then everything that is said about blondes is obviously true.'

The words reached Cynthia across an immense distance, interrupting her retreat from life. The biting cold had faded to nothingness and sleep was just the blink of an eye away.

'Not yet, Goldilocks.' The voice remained tolerant, superior and male. It could have been her father speaking, but he was half the world away in Africa helping others—an old resentment reared weakly, then was gone.

Somewhere, at the far edge of her perception, a small part of Cynthia understood that she was dying, but she was just too tired. In moments, she would be asleep. Her consciousness dwindled to a tiny spark, the sound of his voice and the knowledge that she would never wake were no longer significant.

He would not allow it. 'The time for that is over,' he said, his voice taking on the sternness of her missing parent.

His hand somehow penetrated her sodden clothing to grasp the bare flesh of her shoulder. He was not wearing gloves and his touch was impossibly cold. The intrusion sent a near electric shock through her body. She recoiled from her descent into death and the thin spark of her life flared feebly.

'A hundred paces and you will live through this. Lie there and you will die,' he promised, fingers digging painfully into the muscles of her shoulder as he turned her towards him.

It was the pain that dragged her out of death's embrace, back into a world of icy wind and biting cold. She shuddered violently just as he gripped her left wrist to loop her arm around his neck, her involuntary movement almost pitching him face down in the snow. He staggered then recovered, startling her with a short bark of laughter.

'I am saving your life, Goldilocks. I will not be offended if you decide to help,' he suggested, the dry patronising humour in his voice stirring a distant anger.

She felt his right arm circle her body to grasp the waistband of her ski pants. Then he lifted her bodily, her jacket gaping open at the top and the bottom to funnel the wind through to her sodden thermal underwear. The arctic blast knifed through to her cringing flesh, paring away the layers of lethargy. Hope returned.

She heard someone whimper piteously and an insane fury swept aside all thought.

'Stop whining!' she snarled.

The whimper stopped.

'Good for you, Goldilocks. Get angry. It will help you survive.'

In that distant corner of her mind, where a

small part of Cynthia was still acting as an objective observer, her fear grew, quickly overwhelming hope. Someone had found her, but shelter was impossibly far and he seemed alone. Without help, one death would become two.

She struggled futilely to help, but succeeded only in making his task more difficult as he half-carried, half-dragged her through the deep snow. The thin crust of ice would not support their combined weight and he sank to his waist at each step while her legs floundered helplessly to find a footing on the slick surface.

'Keep those legs moving, Goldilocks,' he urged, his voice cutting through the wind's howl. 'It is not far now.'

To Cynthia, even a single moment more was forever. She could feel herself slipping away, all feeling ebbing from her body. Her rescuer seemed to be tiring and she could hear the desperation in the voice that echoed inside her mind. Worse, she could feel the advance of his fear.

They reached a screen of bushes and he broke through with a lunge that sent them sprawling full length into the sheltered lee of an overhanging rock ledge. Two metres away, yellow light gleamed around the edges of a rough plank door, but her thought processes were now too slow to understand its significance. The interrupted process of dying had taken charge and she was sinking back into the comfort of sleep.

'No!' he roared, as if to hold back the onset of death by sheer volume. 'I will not let you die!'

She felt him stagger to his feet, lifting her with him as he made those few final steps to sanctuary, battering the door aside with his shoulder. The bitter wind became just a sound as she felt herself lowered onto the dry wooden bed of a trolley. As the last tenuous threads of her consciousness unravelled and complete blackness engulfed the tiny spark of life, she felt a rush of pity for him. He had tried so hard and she had let him down.

Awareness came slowly, tentatively; advancing and retreating like gentle waves on a beach. In her confused mind, it was a dream on the edge of reality, totally without physical sensation. Some other Cynthia felt the naked warmth of a hard muscled body pressed against hers; endured the pain of returning circulation to frozen limbs, and had it soothed by the massage with warm eucalypt scented oil. Her only connection lay in the sound of his voice, cajoling, damning, encouraging, and holding her just this side of death.

She was alive! The realisation welled up inside her mind; flooding it with a strange awe. He had succeeded. She was warm. She felt safe. She lay there, unwilling to challenge the miracle of warmth and safety, content just to cherish the miracle of her survival until she was ready to explore her surroundings. Her mind felt fuzzy and reluctant, but there was no physical discomfort.

The silence was the first thing she noticed. It was oddly absolute. Even in the Chalet, she could hear the wind in the trees outside. Here there was nothing; not a single sound of life beyond her own breathing. It felt eerie enough to prompt a tentative exploration of her surroundings.

She lay on her back in a narrow bunk. A soft mattress cushioned her body in warmth and comfort. The throat-catching scent of eucalyptus oil confirmed one of her dreaming memories. She cautiously opened her eyes. Directly above her, someone had hand-carved an intricate crest into the rough-hewn timber of the ceiling. It was upside down from where she lay and unfamiliar, though an uncertain light from her left highlighted the fresh cuts, making them quite distinct. A soft thud and sudden brightening of the light made her turn towards its source. It was the mica-glazed windows of a pot-bellied stove. A piece of wood had settled further into the coals and flared into flame. The increased light partly revealed the shadowed figure of a man drowsing in a strange rustic armchair.

Stretched out towards the stove, his work-scarred lace-up boots were calf-high and topped with a knitted roll of greasy wool. Above that, the roughly woven material of his trousers seemed to absorb the remaining light, leaving the rest of the figure shrouded in darkness. Other than the polished gleam of a large belt buckle at his waist, the only detail she could see was a mass of dark hair drawn back and secured in a thick queue . . .

The archaic term for a man's pigtail came so naturally that it took her a moment to recognise the cause. Everything she could see should have come from a hundred years ago. It was as if they had brought a museum display to life!

An unlit oil lamp, bracketed to the wall next to a shelf of well-used leather-bound books, would light the rough desk, with its capped glass inkstand. A leather miner's cap with a mounted carbide lamp hung beside it. She remembered seeing a similar one in the Long Tunnel Mine museum at Walhalla last summer. This one showed none of the ageing that had made the other look sad rather than functional. Instead, it looked as if he had just put it there after a day's work. An odd flash of visual memory told her that her rescuer had worn it.

It was him! This man had fought for her life and won. Gratitude welled up, tightening her throat muscles and dampening her lashes with tears. She tried to lift her head from the pillow. A wave of weakness surprised her. She closed her eyes against the nausea and felt blindly for something solid to hold onto. The bedclothes rustled, the sound unnaturally loud in the silence.

'You are awake, Goldilocks,' the remembered voice commented and the chair creaked as he came to his feet. She felt, rather than heard, him cross the small room to her side.

'My name is Cynthia Sheldon,' she explained formally, her eyes still tightly closed.

'No "Where am I?" or "What am I doing here?"' he asked, and she could hear the chuckle lurking behind the gentleness in his voice.

'I imagine that you will tell me soon enough. I'm not at the Chalet, nor back at the Stockman's Hut. Therefore, this must be your home.' The nausea was receding, so she opened her eyes cautiously and looked up at her rescuer.

'The lady wins the prize,' he acknowledged, the firelight reflecting on a lean clean-shaven face. 'This is my home for the moment, and you're safe here until the storm blows itself out.'

'It's still blowing? I can't hear it.'

'Not through sixty feet of rock,' he agreed.

The anachronism of using feet instead of metres captured her attention. He seemed to be about her age, possibly a year or two older. That made him thirty at the most. His education should have matched hers. It would have been entirely in metric units. Only an

7

American would have used feet to measure distance and his speech had no trace of an American accent. In fact, he sounded like a well-educated Englishman. His diction and grammar were quite precise. It made the occasional colloquial contraction seem odd.

'You are English,' she accused him.

'No, though I did go Home for the mining degree. There is nothing to match it here.'

The implied criticism of Australia stung. An Anglophile, she thought, raising herself abruptly from the pillow. A move she regretted instantly. Her head spun with the sudden movement. She collapsed back again and closed her eyes tightly as she waited for the bed to stabilise and stop spinning.

'You must take it slowly,' he said. 'You came very close to dying out there. How did you manage to fall through the ice into the creek?'

'We were making a cross-country run from the Stockman's Hut to the Chalet when the weather closed in. I must have missed the turn. We were together one minute. Then, quite suddenly, I was alone. I thought I heard the others and skied towards the sound. The bank gave way and then I was in the water.' She almost shrugged with the simplicity of the disaster that had befallen her. 'How did you find me?'

'I was out checking the vents. A heavy fall can sometimes cover them. I saw the flash of colour across the gully, but it took me over an

8

hour to reach you. I had to open a disused adit to bring you into the mine.'

'We're in a mine?'

'Yes.'

'Oh . . .' Cynthia paused thoughtfully. They were still well within the boundaries of the National Park, giving the clear implication that this was no legal operation, but suggesting this to her rescuer seemed hardly polite.

'What do you mine?' That seemed a safe enough question.

'Gold! The auriferous strata around here are the richest I have ever seen.' A zealot's glow lit his eyes, although his lips curved wryly as he added ruefully, 'They are also the hardest to follow. I sometimes feel that I have chased this reef forever.'

He turned away and crossed the room to the shelf above the desk, returning with a small open-topped canvas bag. As he approached, she could see the glint of gold nuggets. The bag was almost full!

'Look,' he said, shaking a nugget onto the palm of his hand. The size of Cynthia's thumbnail, it was all jagged and rough where it had been broken from the rock. There,were still flecks of marble-like stone sticking to it. 'The mother of all riches.' His tone contained something not unlike awe.

She reached out and took it from the palm of his hand, turning it over in her fingers and admiring its gleam in the firelight. It was surprisingly heavy.

'It is almost pure,' he said. 'I have never seen a seam like it.'

'That bag must be worth a lot of money,' she said, placing the nugget back in his palm. She tried to estimate the weight in the bag and multiply it by the price of gold per ounce.

'Not enough,' he said sadly. 'Unless I strike the main reef, I have not enough to cover costs. It will not keep the bank away from Mitchell's Run.'

'The Drought?' she guessed, recognising the Outback term for a cattle station in the title. A lot of rural properties were in trouble in this third year of below average rainfall.

'Yes,' he agreed. 'That and a pair of land speculators who lifted the hopes of the locals. They spread rumours about the rail line to Sydney.'

Cynthia nodded, remembering the rumours that had accompanied the route of the recent proposal for a high-speed train link to Sydney. It was supposed to replace the century old Melbourne/Sydney rail line. They had favoured two routes, she thought, though she could not remember where they had been supposed to run. A rural family would have found it easy to borrow on the expected increase in price for their land. They would then find themselves deeper in debt than they could ever support with the farm. The son had found another way, one that was not entirely legal. He did not sound like a country boy, but perhaps his parents had been English. It would explain him calling England home.

She lay back in the bed to consider and found her eyelids drooping with a sudden tiredness. Her rescuer reached across and tucked the blankets around her more firmly. The male aroma of sweat, dust and machine oil tickled her nostrils. She could see the glint of red in the hairs on the back of his wrist in the firelight. It all seemed so distant and she felt herself drifting even farther away, though something nagged vaguely at the edge of her consciousness. Her last conscious thought was that brown eyes were much warmer than blue ones.

The smell of food invaded her dreams, twisting them, awakening a hunger so intense as to make sleep impossible. She half-opened her eyes and cautiously raised her head from the pillow. There was no nausea. The scratch of the steel nibbed pen carried clearly across the room and she turned her head towards the sound. Her rescuer was sitting at the desk, writing in a distinctive leather-bound journal by the light of the oil lamp.

'You have decided to rejoin the human race,' he asked, apparently alerted by her movement in the bed.

'If that's the price of being fed,' she agreed, opening her eyes fully and sitting up. The movement halted abruptly as she realised that

11

she was naked under the bedclothes.

'Your clothes are on the end of the bed. They are dry now,' he said.

He rose from the desk and walked out through the doorway to her left, near the head of the bed, leaving her with the distinct impression that his eyes had lingered for more than a moment on her exposed body.

She flushed uncomfortably. Then her memory rebuked her. He had undressed her, dried her, and warmed her with the heat of his naked body before massaging the circulation into her limbs. He had already seen everything at his leisure. The fading scent of eucalyptus oil clung to the bedclothes to remind her of all he had done for her. It was churlish to begrudge him a typical male reaction.

She turned away from the door and looked down at the foot of the bed. Just as he said, her clothing lay folded neatly, with her thermal underwear on top. She reached for the latter. The cabin was warm enough for the quilted outer clothing to be superfluous. She slid into the cellular vest and long johns. Their weave was dense enough to protect her modesty and they were warmed by the fire and totally dry. A shake of her head and a quick comb with her fingers made her hair as presentable as it was ever going to be and she was ready for food. Her bare feet slid easily into the well-used moccasins he had left conveniently at the side of the bed, but she found them big enough that

12

she had to shuffle rather than walk. It did not delay her; the aromas coming through the door and her hunger made the difficulty inconsequential.

She found the next room a combined kitchen and eating area, lit by an oil lamp with a tall, sparklingly clean glass chimney. A large wood stove took up most of one wall and a scrubbed pine table the other. There was only one chair, another rustic construction, well polished by use, which would have fetched a small fortune at any art auction. He motioned her towards it, ladled a thick, rich smelling stew into a tin bowl and placed it before her. Waiting on the table was a large, fresh damper. Beside it a ceramic crock of butter, rich and yellow—obviously not factory-made.

'We are deficient in cutlery,' he explained. 'You can have the spoon and I will make do with the fork.'

'I don't even know your name,' she said, politeness briefly battling her hunger.

'Andrew Mitchell.'

She nodded her acknowledgment, her mouth far too busy with the process of eating to make a verbal response. The stew was superb, even allowing for her hunger. It held flavours that she could not recognise, but each complemented the other so well that the result made them individually unimportant. It was not until she was wiping the last scraps from the bowl with a large piece of damper that she felt impelled to continue the conversation.

'This is very good,' she said unnecessarily. 'You could be a cordon bleu cook.'

'I suspect hunger added to its quality for you, but, as I am the one that has to eat it normally, I prefer that I can enjoy it as well,' Andrew explained.

He was at the stove, looking at her over his shoulder. A rare smile briefly softened his features. He seemed amused by her, as if her reactions were slightly off-key. She abruptly remembered his remark about blondes when he found her in the snow. She would make him pay for that . . . gently of course. She might owe him her life, but no man treated her as a dumb blonde with impunity.

He turned back to the table, holding a pot of tea and a chipped, but spotlessly clean, china mug.

'I will use the pannikin,' he explained, placing the mug before her. 'I usually do when I am working. I am afraid we have no milk. I've got used to doing without it.'

Black unsweetened tea was not one of her favourite drinks, but she enjoyed it none the less. Her situation was unique. Few ate a meal deep in an undoubtedly illegal mine in the middle of a blizzard in an Alpine National Park and drank tea from a mug emblazoned with a regimental crest. She took a deep sip and placed the mug carefully on the table as she looked directly at her host for the

14

first time.

Andrew Mitchell was very impressive. At least 185 centimetres tall, he had a lean athletic body without a gram of excess fat. Even in rough working clothes, he had a sense of 'rightness' about him that suggested he could wear any outfit well. Strangely, perhaps because of the military insignia on the mug in her hand, she could picture him easily in an old-fashioned cavalry uniform. Immaculate, dashing, with bright brass buttons and bullion epaulettes. There was that military vitality of an energetic man of action in his movements. Yet, in his face, there was the look of a dreamer. Something about his expression suggested a love of far places and distant horizons. Perhaps it was the focus of his eyes. A brown so dark as to appear almost black in the soft lamplight, they seemed able to see through her and beyond, as if he were looking into her future—or her past. She shook herself free of her fey imaginings and returned to the present.

'Is the storm over yet?'

'It is still blowing a full gale. Sleet has closed the whole mountain range. Visibility was less than twenty feet an hour ago. When this stops it will snow quite heavily. We will have only the short break between to get you back to your friends.'

'They will have given up on me,' Cynthia said. 'It's a pity that we can't contact them,' she continued, a question in her tone.

'The Alpine people will hope that you have been lucky,' he responded non-committally. 'This is the second day that you have been missing. They know the odds.'

'They know you're here . . .' she asked, taking the obvious inference from his words while she mentally acknowledged the reason for her unusually sharpened appetite.

Not everyone. Most believe that I am just a myth,' he answered obliquely.

'Do you play chess?' he asked, changing the subject. 'The weather will not break until late this evening. I will get you back to the Chalet when it happens, but we have nearly seven hours to fill.'

Cynthia nodded, remembering smugly the school and university tournaments she had won. It was her chance to show him she was no dumb blonde, though she would have to be careful not to win too easily. A woman beating him might just offend her host. Most men were still chauvinists when it came to contests with women.

They moved back into the other room and she sat on the bed while he occupied the armchair, the chessboard resting on a small stool between them. The chess pieces themselves were sturdy, plain, and polished by much use. When she won the use of the white, she opened with the standard central development, easily maintaining tempo through the first half dozen moves. At that point, she exposed her weakness, a tendency to rely too much on the power of her queen. He curbed her sharply with a well-supported Knight defence, forcing her to retreat in disorder. From then on, she battled to regain tempo. When that failed, she struggled to survive a relentless attack. In the end, he allowed her to force a stalemate. A deliberate act, she suspected. She could not help but challenge the implied condescension.

'You let me off with a stalemate,' she accused.

'You played well, and you are my guest,' he agreed obliquely.

'Then I deserve the courtesy of an honest game.'

'I suspect you will always demand a man's best effort,' he said, eyeing her levelly without challenge. 'We have the time to play another game. Would you like to be white again?'

'No,' she said. 'It's your turn to have the advantage.'

The quirk at the corner of his smile made her realise how ungracious that sounded. She felt a warm flush of embarrassment, but could think of no way to retrieve her blunder, so she busied herself with the chessboard, turning it around to take advantage of the pieces already in place. The board caught the edge of the chair and the white queen toppled over and rolled off the edge. They both grabbed for it, but she was faster and his hand closed over her fingers as they held the chess piece. Once more, his touch was electric and she jerked her hand back before she could control the reaction.

He smiled at her and held out his open hand, palm up. 'I think I might need that,' he said. 'You are too good for me to give you that much start.'

She flushed and placed the white queen in his hand. He paused, looking down at the chess piece as if he had never seen it before. Then he turned it over and looked at its base before looking up at her. It was as if he had suddenly stepped back to consider what was happening from an impartial viewpoint. She endured his moment of judgement for a small eternity before he looked down again and positioned the white queen on the chessboard. He made his first move as soon as all the pieces were in place and the game began.

His opening followed an obscure pattern at the King's Rook end of the board. She had read about it, but never seen it played before. His subtle embellishments to what she had read kept her off-balance well into the middle game. Beyond that, it was only dogged defence that allowed her to survive, move by move, until finally forced to concede defeat. She resigned her king to his overwhelming development and strength, conceding that his tactics had led her inevitably to this point.

There was an odd comfort in acknowledging that she had played her best game, but a better player had won.

She looked up and caught his measuring study of her features. There was that same sense that she had done something outside of his expectation. He seemed both amused and intrigued, but he did not look away, just smiled at her, awakening something dormant in the pit of her stomach.

In the third game, she regained control of the board and the white pieces. She stuck to the standard opening, for he had proved himself far too good a player for her to experiment. He matched her development, constantly threatening any mistake with a loss of tempo, and she had to concentrate totally on the game. She found herself reluctant to look at her host. The context of his scrutiny between games had woken something quite distracting. She even wondered briefly whether it had been deliberate. She had used the same sort of gamesmanship to destroy an obnoxious opponent in a tournament and Andrew had already shown himself capable of extreme subtlety. With him, she could take nothing at face value.

Even with that warning, she missed the sly shift in focus that gave him the game in three swift forked attacks.

'You are a very worthy opponent,' he congratulated her, sitting back into his chair as she tilted her king onto its side and acknowledged a second defeat.

'I think you outclassed me,' she admitted honestly, her eyes bright with the zest of battle—and something else she chose not to define.

She held the white king in her hand, her fingers idly exploring a crack in its crown until the symbolism of its shape and what she was doing suddenly dawned on her and she put it down hurriedly. The situation was now totally beyond her control, not unlike the three chess games. It was an odd experience for Cynthia.

He was smiling quite broadly now and the twinkle in his eye was pure mischief. It made Cynthia suddenly aware that they were alone in the privacy of his home. It did not feel threatening. After all, this man had saved her life. She could have no compunction in allowing him whatever reward he wanted—her body included. There should be time enough, she thought, if they could trust his original estimate. Her heart beat accelerated and she felt her body stir in preparation. Her lips grew unaccountably dry and she wet them nervously with the tip of her tongue.

He laughed abruptly, the same brief bark of humour that had startled her in the snow. 'This has become pure Music Hall farce,' he said. 'It is not my style. I do not want gratitude.'

Although she sensed that he was rebuking

himself rather than her, the words, none the less, were a slap in the face and she recoiled in embarrassment. It was as if he could read her thoughts.

He stilled her response, holding up his left hand, palm towards her, as a command, as he appeared to listen to some variation in the silence that only he could detect.

'In any case, it is time to get you back to your friends. As soon as you are into your clothes, we must go,' he said, scooping the chessmen into their box and returning them and the board to the desk.

He allowed her no time to think, let alone argue, as he hurried her into her outer clothing. He even knelt to strap on her boots, managing the clips with more ease than she could ever achieve. Once she was ready, his preparations took seconds. He shrugged his way into a horseman's oilskin coat that reached down to his calves, lit the lamp on the miner's cap and closed its glass cover. Then he hustled her out of the cabin, pausing only to extinguish the kerosene lamps.

They emerged into a dark tunnel, lit only by the lamp in his cap. She glanced back regretfully at the cabin and followed reluctantly; half-blinded by tears she could not comfortably explain. The tunnel walls seemed very close and she stumbled over steel rail-tracks visible only by the tops worn bright with use.

'Keep to the left,' he instructed. 'There is a path on that side.'

They passed through a larger chamber, skirted the opening of a vertical shaft as they turned right to enter another tunnel. This one sloped gently upwards. When they finally emerged, it was into a cave high on the mountain slope. Outside, in the darkening fall of night, scattered flurries of snow were falling. The wind was now blustering playfully rather than blasting its way across the roof of the Victorian Alps.

Her skis, stocks and backpack were there, leaning against a winch bolted to the cave floor. He must have returned to the creek for them while she slept. Andrew lay the skis in the snow near the entrance and knelt to attach her bindings and check the tension as she stepped into them. She took advantage of his distraction to dry her eyes with the lining of her gloves. It was cold enough outside to freeze her tears.

'Come,' he said, standing up. 'We must hurry now.' He started to turn away and stopped, obviously remembering something. 'Here,' he said, turning back and extending his hand to her. 'You will need this.'

She had lost the brightly coloured beanie as she fell through the ice. It was now a little battered. The pompom on the top was missing and he had obviously rolled it in the pocket of his coat, but it was dry. She pulled it well down so that it covered most of the honey blonde glory that was her hair. He watched her with an odd expression in his eyes. In the light from his cap lamp, reflected off the walls of the mine entrance, his expression was almost sad. He appeared to regret the need for haste, storing a picture of her in his mind for the future.

He turned away abruptly and stepped into the old-fashioned bindings on a set of skis that must have been a hundred years old. After checking that she was ready, he led off to break the trail, the long coat tails of his oilskins flapping in each gust. The glow of his lamp, reflected from the snow, made it easy for her to keep him in sight and she followed exactly in his trail.

It seemed an endless journey. The darkness hid everything familiar from her sight, making it feel as if they were travelling more through time than distance. Yet Andrew seemed to know precisely where he was going, following the contours to make the climb easier, choosing a path to avoid the undergrowth, breaking a trail that allowed her to keep up. He kept his pace just within her ability by checking often, glancing over his shoulder and adjusting his tempo to the slope to keep her two ski lengths behind.

The mindlessness of following in his tracks gave her time to think . . . and feel a little ashamed.

Andrew Mitchell had compromised a profitable illegal operation to save her life, risking his own in the process. He had given her a lesson in chess, tolerated her pettiness and then refused to take advantage of her gratitude. This was a very rare man. It was up to her to find a way of repaying him that he would accept . . . and he would find that she did not give up easily.

It came as a surprise when he stopped at the crest of a ridge and swung his skis until they were pointing back along their tracks and waited for her to reach him. She stopped with her skis parallel to his, but facing the other way so that they stood right shoulder to right shoulder.

'The lights of the Chalet,' he said, extending his right arm to point down the slope before her. 'Just follow the ski run. I can go no further than this. It is now time for me to return.'

Cynthia, struggling to bring her breathing back to normal, remained silent, breathing as deeply as she could.

'I have two souvenirs for you,' he continued. 'This,' he took the nugget she had examined from his pocket and tucked it into the zippered top pocket of her jacket, 'is for the others. It will prove that it actually happened . . . and this is for you. I want to make certain that you remember me.' With that he swept her into his arms and kissed her.

Cynthia cooperated very enthusiastically. If

he was prepared to accept a kiss, she was more than prepared to make it the best she was able to give. She surrendered totally to the moment, allowing herself to become pliant as his arms held her firmly against a body hard with the physical labour of mining. She could taste the herbs he had used on the stew and tannin bite of the black tea on his tongue, but his lips were surprisingly gentle on hers. This man would take only what she ceded willingly.

It was just a very pleasant experience, although she damned the thick winter clothes for their interference, until the memory of his naked body against hers was suddenly very intense. Her need for him flared, becoming a furnace that would have consumed her utterly, had he not chosen that moment to break their embrace and push her gently away.

It left Cynthia teetering uncertainly on her skis, disoriented by the interruption to the message she was sending. His voice seemed to come from a distance . . .

'It is time for you to go back to your world. Do not forget me too easily. I know that I will never forget you. You are the most beautiful thing I have ever seen. Goodbye, Goldilocks.' He pushed off with his stocks and accelerated smoothly down the reverse slope away from her. She stared after him, physically drained by the brief burst of passion, incapable of any action other than to watch him leave, acutely conscious of her disappointment.

It was only when the glow from his cap lamp had faded completely that she realised her own danger. The snowfalls were increasing rapidly and the diffused loom of the chalet lights was barely visible. Soon she would have nothing to guide her. She sighed gently, set off cautiously, and skied steadily down the hill, returning reluctantly to her own world.

The police station was her first call. They would be coordinating the search and she owed them the duty of reporting her return. It would also be the first test of her determination to protect Andrew Mitchell. He had not asked her to conceal his presence, but she must do everything that she could to hide his part in her rescue.

A tall blonde female Senior Constable was on desk duty. She took down all the details on a printed report sheet; an odd expression flitting across her face occasionally, particularly when Cynthia nervously over-explained the points that concealed Andrew Mitchell's involvement. It was surprisingly hard to lie deliberately, no matter how honourable her intentions.

When the report was complete, the policewoman insisted on escorting Cynthia to the Alpine Patrol Headquarters. The duty Patrol Commander was in the midst of planning a day of scaled down searching, convinced that she was already dead. Nothing would satisfy him short of another recital of her escape. She kept her description of the terrain vague, pleading darkness and ignorance, saying that she had stumbled on the trail to the village by accident. It was the best she could do for her rescuer.

'You have been very lucky,' the Patrol Commander commented. 'Very few people have survived forty-eight hours in those sort of conditions without help. Your initiative in finding a cave and using it so effectively is commendable.'

Cynthia flushed, knowing how little she deserved his praise. She was about to leave the small office when she noticed a large newssheet under glass on the wall. It was the front page of a newspaper and, taking up the full page, was a recognisable picture of her rescuer!

'That's Andrew Mitchell. Our last hope was that you had met him.' The Patrol Commander had noted her sharp focus. 'He is a legend up here, that some of us have been forced to accept.' He gave the policewoman a hard look, suggesting that she was not a believer.

Cynthia hardly heard him. She was staring at the date on the top of the page. It was impossible! It claimed that Andrew Mitchell disappeared on August 21st, 1886!

2

Three months later, as Cynthia drove over the cattle grid at the entrance to Mitchell's Run, the thump of the tyres on the individual bars was almost as loud as the beating of her heart. She was incredibly nervous. When she left Melbourne, five hours earlier, what she intended had seemed reasonable. It now felt foolish. Worse, it could embarrass both her and the man who had pretended to be Andrew Mitchell.

She had been the victim of an elaborate hoax perpetrated to protect an illegal gold mine. It was the only acceptable explanation. Ghosts do not have bodies, let alone body-warmth to combat hypothermia. They can not pass physical objects, like gold nuggets, from their world to hers. She had felt his warmth and had the nugget in her pocket. Therefore, she would face the hoaxer, thank him for her life, do whatever she could to repay her debt and close the incident.

A simple goal—unfortunately determined largely by others, particularly her father.

He had arrived from aid agency headquarters in Africa the morning after her return to the Chalet. Intrigued by the story of her rescue, he set in motion an investigation into Andrew Mitchell. Since then, he had followed its progress in detail, discussing it with Cynthia each time that he rang home. The succession of Andrew Mitchells since 1886 seemed preposterous at first—more suitable to cheap romantic fiction than reality. However, the steady accumulation of evidence had shown a deliberate pattern of succession, even to the choice of career. Something very odd was going on in the Mitchell family. She was not sure what it was, but she intended to find out. In any case, a conscientious search for the truth was a more acceptable excuse than the memory of a single kiss.

Yet she may still have let the matter drop were it not for a segment of a life-style program on television covering the bed and breakfast inn the Mitchell family operated at the old homestead, north of Omeo. Drew Mitchell appeared in the background only briefly, but long enough to leave no doubt in Cynthia's mind that he was the man who had rescued her from the snow.

When Cynthia still hesitated, Jo Sanderson intervened and booked an overnight stay at the B&B. Jo had been Cynthia's best friend since childhood. She was confidante, constant companion, staunch ally to Cynthia's father, Edward Sheldon, and an incurable romantic as well as the design genius behind the fashion boutique she and Cynthia operated jointly in South Yarra. She would not take no for an answer, coercing Cynthia into going in her place and leaving her to explain the substitution as a simple change of plans.

Drew Mitchell would be there. Jo had spoken to him while making the booking, flirted outrageously and extracted a promise to see her on arrival.

Cynthia arrived just after five, as planned. She had left Melbourne at noon and taken her time, particularly on the road north from Bairnsdale. It ran close to the river for some of the way and the mountain scenery was fabulous. At Omeo, she had stopped briefly to ask directions. Mitchell's Run lay off the main road north to Tallangatta, which ran up the far side of the Bogong High Plains from where she had become lost.

From the gate, she could not see the house; just a well made driveway leading up through an open stand of trees along the ridge in front of her. When she reached the ridge top, she discovered that a curved dam wall bridged the broad gully beyond it to create an ornamental lake in front of the homestead—a cluster of buildings straddling the crest of a second ridge. The main house was typical of the area, built of dressed local granite in the style of yesteryear, with a wide verandah on all sides. The driveway continued along the top of the dam wall and led to a covered parking area just to the left of the front door. A discreet sign identified this as Guest Parking. Cynthia took the space closest to the house and got out of her car.

Her nervousness had grown to the point where she was very close to an undignified retreat.

'Jo Sanderson?'

Cynthia started uncontrollably and turned towards the verandah at the sound of the woman's voice. Dulcie Tennant, her host for the evening, was obviously a Mitchell by birth. The family resemblance to Andrew Mitchell was strong. She matched Cynthia for height, but had none of her soft curves. Whipcord and fine leather were the similes that sprang to Cynthia's mind. Dulcie had a country look, body and skin toughened by the elements and hard work.

'J-Jo could not make it at the last minute, so I decided to come instead,' Cynthia explained, the slight stutter at the beginning making her flush uncomfortably. 'My name is Cynthia Sheldon. I do hope that you don't mind,' she ended anxiously

'Not at all,' Dulcie assured her, a slight pause almost unnoticeable. 'You are our only guest tonight, please come in and I'll show you to your room.'

Cynthia found herself settled into the main bedroom at the southern end of the house. It overlooked the lake and the valley to the east and had an adjoining toilet and shower. She unpacked and freshened herself at Dulcie's invitation, then joined the other woman in the kitchen for a cup of tea and some country scones. Dulcie was in the middle of cooking, she explained, and the kitchen was warmer, but Cynthia suspected the older woman was trying to put her at ease. She must have seemed very nervous to her host, jumping so obviously at the sound of her voice.

They were on the second cup and chatting comfortably when Drew Mitchell entered the room. He saw Cynthia and stopped dead.

Triumph flared in Cynthia's mind. He was, beyond doubt, her rescuer in the flesh and his shock was all the confirmation that she needed. She relaxed a little, no longer concerned that she was making a fool of herself.

He had been to a barber since she saw him last and his hair had more reddish tints than she remembered, but that was probably the effect of the late afternoon sunlight. He had replaced the old-fashioned working clothes with well-worn jeans and a faded plaid cotton shirt. Both had shrunk slightly with repeated washing and left no doubt of the lean strength of his body.

Drew poured himself a country mug of tea and stole two of the scones Dulcie had prepared for herself, well layered with jam and clotted cream. As he distracted Dulcie from the act of theft, he winked at Cynthia, almost making her choke on a mouthful. It made him seem so much younger than he had at the mine. There was more than a touch of the larrikin in Drew Mitchell, the man who had called himself Andrew in the mine.

He was also erudite, witty, charming and perceptive—qualities he demonstrated beyond doubt as they sat in the sun-warmed kitchen in the northern corner of the house. Dulcie ceded him the duties of host, as if these were his rights, but it did not stop her giving him chore after chore with laughing authority.

'The devil makes use of idle hands,' she said to Cynthia, as if justifying the need to keep him occupied.

'So it would seem,' Drew agreed, finishing off the last of the scones. 'I knew it was only a matter of time before you lot claimed the role of Satan as well as God.'

'Get out of here and shower, you chauvinist. Dinner will be at seven. I want the fire set in the small dining room, the table set for three, and pads for four warming dishes,' Dulcie instructed.

'Yes, Missus. No, Missus. Three bags full, Missus.'

Drew's ear for accent was obviously as good as his eye for detail. He subtly exaggerated his imitation of an outback rouseabout to accentuate the insolence of the last phrase as he backed out of the kitchen.

The room seemed empty when he left.

Cynthia excused herself shortly after, retrieved a warm jacket from her room and set out to follow the white gravel path that circled the lake.

In spite of three years of near drought conditions, the water was at its design level. An ornamental stone tower, linked to the shore by a narrow wooden bridge, concealed the spillway that kept it there, balancing the flow of the spring high in the mountains behind the homestead. The whole thing was a construction of considerable engineering merit, according to the sign at the lake edge, and attributed to the original Andrew Mitchell.

Cynthia had stayed at B&Bs throughout the world and the operating brain behind this one was obviously astute. Dulcie maintained the homely atmosphere, but a host of professional touches lay in the covered guest parking, the informative signs, and the immaculately maintained grounds. Nothing detracted from the setting, nor jarred the eye. It was a tasteful conversion of a well loved home into an effective business.

Cynthia finished half the circuit of the lake and stood among the trees looking to the east and the peaks that still caught the sunlight. It was a beautiful sight. One she would not forget quickly. It was no wonder that Drew Mitchell fought so hard to retain this place. She turned away and looked across the lake at the homestead, shadowed by the mountains behind, but still distinct. It had a timeless quality, not unlike some of the buildings she had seen in Europe, and a sense of rightness that justified any effort to keep it that way.

She was glad that she had come to Mitchell's Run. It explained many things.

The sound of a dinner gong interrupted her thoughts and she completed the circuit of the lake and went inside the house thankfully. The mountains to the west hid the sun and it was growing cold, even with her jacket.

Drew was stoking the open fire in the small dining room, kneeling before it as he added split red gum to the bed of coals, arranging each piece so that it would fall into the coals as it burnt. The fire had already warmed the room to the point where Cynthia could discard her jacket. Drew came to his feet as she entered and moved to help her, taking her jacket and hanging it on a stand just inside the door. He then ushered her to a place set near the head of the table, drawing back the chair for her. The ambience of Mitchell's Run made his actions seem natural.

Dulcie came in with the last of the four serving dishes and sat down opposite Cynthia, leaving Drew the place at the head of the table. The deference was subtle, but unmistakable. In spite of his relative youth, Drew Mitchell was undoubtedly the head of the Mitchell clan. There was an almost feudal feel to the arrangement.

'Jack and Peter are away at Mansfield,

setting up for the race meeting,' Dulcie explained as Drew sat down. 'That's why there are only the three of us tonight.'

The meal was superlative. Good cooking was clearly a dominant gene in the Mitchell family; and Drew was the perfect host, drawing out Cynthia's background, particularly the operation of a South Yarra fashion boutique. Dulcie then discussed the current trends with a far more intimate knowledge than Cynthia would have expected of a woman living exclusively in the country. Drew added a comment here and there, but seemed content to let Dulcie carry the conversation now that he had drawn their guest into speaking.

Cynthia raised the subject of Andrew Mitchell to change that. She wanted to listen to Drew's voice. It seemed different from her memory of how it had sounded in the mine.

'Drew is our resident expert on the subject of our Andrew,' Dulcie said. 'If he doesn't know, I doubt that the information is available.'

Which was only to be expected, Cynthia thought. His masquerade in the mine was letter perfect. She looked across the table and saw the mischief in his eyes. He was enjoying the situation, guessing how tempted she was to blurt out her knowledge of his masquerade in the mine, yet content to wait for his moment. Her time would come and they would see how much he enjoyed being on the receiving end.

'Andrew Mitchell seems very important to this place. It is almost as if he was still alive?'

Drew's grin was a wicked acknowledgment of her sly dig. 'I suppose we should satisfy you,' he said blandly, composing his features into a semblance of innocence. He then summarised the known history of Andrew Mitchell as if Cynthia were just a guest who had expressed interest.

Andrew had been the youngest of four brothers. The only one not to stay on the land, he had been the epitome of the Victorian Gentleman. He had stopped in South Africa on his return from studying in England, joining an American prospector to follow up rumours of gold at Johannesburg. Instead, he became embroiled in the Zulu war. Fighting his way clear of the massacre at Isandlwhana, then standing with the others at Rorke's Drift. A superb horseman, his exploits in Africa and at home had been the basis for half a dozen bush ballads in the old *Bulletin* magazine. Banjo Paterson, the weekly paper's most famous writer, had written some of them. There were even theories that Andrew was the model for Paterson's poem, 'The Man from Snowy River' rather than Jim Craig, as the popular film claimed.

'Did Paterson ever meet him,' she asked, unaccountably irritated by the admiration in Drew's voice.

'Yes, they were both at Sydney Grammar,

though ten years apart, and shared an interest in horse racing. Both rode successfully as amateur jockeys. Paterson is reputed to have urged him not to go to the Sudan with the Australian troops against the Mahdi. So they must have met again after Andrew returned from South Africa,' he explained, before returning to the story of his ancestor.

Andrew came back when his brothers had fallen into financial difficulties. They had speculated on land for the railway line between Melbourne and Albury, part of the link to Sydney. A pair of land agents had tolled them in deliberately. They planned to get the land of Mitchell's Run for a pittance when the brothers failed. He had horsewhipped the two agents publicly in a Sydney street, coldly humiliating them with a stockwhip, before tongue lashing his brothers in private—younger brother or no. To save Mitchell's Run he had done a deal with their creditors, then gone up into the high country and found enough gold to keep them at bay. Three times, he had met their demands. The fourth time he had not returned and half the land had gone, tearing the heart out of Mitchell's Run. It had never recovered, declining slowly until it was just a memory in the minds of the Mitchell family and the older mountain cattlemen. Many had voiced dark suspicions at the time that the two land speculators had sent paid thugs to kill him, but no one could prove it.

'Do you think that is what happened,' she asked, fascinated by the amplification of the story she already knew.

'I'd doubt it,' he scoffed. 'Andrew was a Bushman and an ex-army scout. Its unlikely that any city thug could have surprised him . . . and no one who met him face to face would have survived. He had rather stringent views on people who attacked him, or the family.'

Cynthia was now very puzzled. Drew had relaxed completely telling the story that must have been as familiar to him as his own life. It was obvious that he admired Andrew. He had already proved that he was a superb actor and that he could play his part in masquerading as the long dead miner. Yet this was not the man she had met in the mine. His voice seemed different, but that could be explained by his talent for mimicry. It was something beyond that, some inherent difference that she could only sense. Her certainties were fading a little and she wondered anew if she was not making a fool of herself.

Dulcie rose from her chair, went to the sideboard for the coffee, and served them all, leaving the glass percolator jug on the warming tray where they could all reach it for refills. There was a twinkle in her eyes, as if something amused her.

Cynthia suspected that it was Drew. He was being very charming.

She had grown up with the knowledge that

39

her appearance had an odd effect on men, rendering them blind to its defects. On his last brief visit, her father had called Cynthia 'a classic honey-blonde' and 'a Vargas postcard brought to life'. She had not believed the first description, nor recognised the second reference until she found a collection of Alberto Vargas' pin-up girls in an art book. They all appeared to have impossibly long legs and one thought on their minds so the comparison was hardly flattering.

Her attitude to her own appearance was ambivalent, a mixture of intellectual acceptance without real conviction. The effects were too consistent for her to ignore, but she did not feel beautiful. External evidence made her accept it, but could not make her really believe it.

It obviously interested Drew . . . just as it had interested Andrew.

It was a flattering situation; either she had attracted the attention of two very interesting men . . . or one very complex man. She hoped that it was the latter. A choice between the two would be impossible.

'Another coffee?' Dulcie was still the perfect hostess. 'We have some very good port?'

'One more mouthful of anything and I shall burst,' Cynthia replied. 'I would count the cost of driving here a very small price for a meal like this. Jo said she was lucky to get a booking and I can understand why.' Her compliments were the truth. Mitchell's Run was a place to which people would return just to enjoy the food.

'There is no wind tonight and the moon is full. Bring your jacket and I will walk you around the lake,' Drew offered, a gleam in his eye that had little to do with mischief.

'An offer too good to refuse,' Cynthia agreed, rising from her chair and waiting for Drew to remove it so she could step clear of the table.

Such courtesies were natural at Mitchell's Run, for this was not just a recreation of the past. It was the continuation of an earlier age, maintained faithfully by people who still believed. Drew did not disappoint her. He even held her jacket, and smiled with pleasure at the privilege.

'Breakfast will be at eight,' Dulcie said. 'I'm off to bed as soon as I clean up, so I will see you then.'

Cynthia nodded her acceptance of the arrangement; her mind on more immediate matters as her body remembered the kiss on the mountain. She was oddly certain that Drew would kiss her by the lake and quietly content with the prospect. It seemed natural that he should continue from their parting on the mountain, regardless of the months that lay between.

The gravel of the path gleamed whitely in the moonlight, making Cynthia think of a

41

magical road through the darkness. The stand of trees that had hidden the homestead from the gate did little to interrupt her view of the valley, particularly when they reached the far side of the lake.

'In Andrew's day, Mitchell's Run took in the whole of the valley. We owned all the land that you can see,' he explained, the sweep of his arm encompassing the visible horizon. 'Now the cattle gate you drove through is the eastern limit. There is only the homestead and the lake.'

She turned towards him expectantly. He had chosen a perfect setting to continue the moment on the mountain and she was impatient—her moment of triumph had arrived. There was a brief hesitation on his part, then their bodies merged in a kiss, the past glories of Mitchell's Run forgotten.

It was the moment on the mountain all over again. Her doubts fled with the familiarity of his embrace. No two men could kiss like this, nor feel so much the same in her arms. She surrendered completely once more. It was like coming home.

Drew ended the kiss this time as well. Cynthia would have let it go on forever. She felt their lips part and her eyes opened. He was smiling at her.

'As you can see, I did not forget you,' she said. It was time to enjoy her triumph.

The smile left his face. 'Andrew rescued you

earlier this year. The local paper covered the story, although their photograph did not do you justice,' he said, his tone even, his expression unreadable in the moonlight.

'The paper said nothing about Andrew Mitchell,' she accused, her doubts resurfacing as anger with his stubborn refusal to accept that she knew the truth of his masquerade.

'To anyone, who knew the area, your story had more holes than a colander. It was obvious that you had run into him, otherwise you would have died.' His tone was dismissive, as if her persistence disappointed him.

'I kept your secret from the police and the Alpine Patrol. I said I had sheltered in a cave,' Cynthia assured him, ignoring his attempt to divert her, anxious to confirm her discretion after he left her on the mountain.

'It's a great pity the man's dead,' he said musingly, 'God knows Goldilocks, I envy him his success with the ladies.'

'There!' she challenged. 'You called me Goldilocks on the mountain as well.'

'The dark-haired males in our family have a historical tendency towards blonde women. By tradition, they call them all Goldilocks. I have no doubt Andrew called you exactly that. Did you play chess as well?'

'Yes,' she admitted, a little uncertainly. The control of the conversation kept slipping away from her and that something about his voice that did not fit her memory kept nagging

43

at her.

'Did you win?'

'You allowed me to stalemate the first game, but you won the next two.'

'You did better than most. He was champion of the colony and undefeated at Oxford.'

'I don't suppose you play at all,' she accused, counterattacking to throw him off-balance.

'On the contrary, I play very well. It's another family tradition,' he responded, blithely ignoring her attack.

'Are you really trying to tell me that you are not the man who rescued me and gave me this?' she said, thrusting him away and taking the nugget from her jacket pocket. She held it out towards him.

'That's a first. He has never shared his gold before. You must have really impressed him,' he answered her obliquely. Not entirely unlike the way he had answered unwanted questions in the mine.

'Don't play with me,' she warned. 'I don't understand why you won't admit the truth. I've already said that I don't care that you are mining illegally in a national park.'

'Twice now,' he agreed blandly.

'Then stop being obstinate and admit to the truth.'

'Whose truth would you like me to admit to, yours or mine?'

44

She almost snorted in exasperation. As either Andrew or Drew, this man was the most elusive she had ever met. He had to be lying! There was no other acceptable explanation. Yet he kept denying obvious facts. She was positive that he was deliberately playing with her, particularly when she abruptly identified the difference in his voice. He had been very subtle. The timbre and the tone he had left unchanged. All he had done was relax the precision of his speech, allowing the inclusion of more colloquial contractions. He now sounded like a well educated Australian rather than an Englishman. He was very good at it, not quite good enough to fool her, but still very good.

Drew had stepped back and stood a long pace away from her, his face unshadowed in the moonlight. 'You are accusing me of rescuing you on the mountain, then pretending to be Andrew to hide the fact that I was mining for gold illegally within a national park,' he paused, a dramatic action slightly overdone. 'Don't you find that a little far-fetched?' Drew accented his question with an inquiring lift of one eyebrow and a wry grin.

'The alternative is a ghost with physical powers beyond anything I've ever read about,' Cynthia countered. She was more than capable of holding her own against this sort of attack.

'You haven't heard of Andrew's other exploits then?'

'I have read the reports of the other rescues attributed to him,' she admitted.

'Most of them happened before I was born,' he observed mildly.

'You have had an Andrew Mitchell in every generation of your family. None of them has been a direct descendant of the other, but all of them have borne a remarkable resemblance to the original. All, bar one, have been mining engineers interested in gold. The one exception was a soldier who reportedly died in the Western Desert during the Second World War. That is taking tradition a little too far, even for a family who seem to pay more than lip service to the past.'

'You've done your research well. Just what are you suggesting? A family tradition of masquerades . . . or some form of reincarnation? Perhaps you believe that I was born in 1854?'

'I know that is nonsense. You have a proper birth certificate and an admirable academic record.'

'That does not rule out reincarnation.'

'The dates are wrong. All the successive generations of Andrew Mitchells have coexisted for some part of their lives. Your uncle was at your christening and you were at his funeral. You came back from England to attend it.'

'How did you accumulate all this information in three months?'

'I paid for it mostly. I did the initial inquiries and became curious, so I paid people to do the rest,' she said coldly, a growing anger trapping her into taking the credit for her father's actions.

'You are a very determined lady, Goldilocks,' he said. A matching anger in his voice gave the nickname a derisive sound. 'It seems a strange way to repay a debt.'

Her anger blossomed into a sudden rage that caught Cynthia by surprise. All her doubts and the frustration of nothing quite going to plan boiled up inside her. 'Please do not treat me as if I were just a dumb blonde,' she blazed, just managing to control her voice this side of shrillness. 'I am not stupid! I do not believe in ghosts. Even if I did, it was a man who rescued me on the mountain. He was flesh and blood, just as you and I.' She paused, took a deep breath and continued. 'You saved my life. I do not care what you were doing there. I just want to thank you and do whatever I can to repay my debt; then I can get on with the rest of my life.'

Drew Mitchell stood quietly for a few moments, studying her face with a curious air of detachment that was acutely familiar. Like the moment in the mine between games, it was as if he were more an observer than a participant.

When he finally spoke, his tone was quietly conversational . . . 'I suppose that this is my cue to confess all of my sins, and the sins of my family, so that your absurd romantic daydream can become a reality?' He paused, looked at Cynthia with an air of mild inquiry, and then continued, more firmly. 'Well, Goldilocks, I am afraid you must be satisfied with the public version of the tale. A ghost rescued you on the high plains. As for what you have discovered about my family, I do not intend to explain, or to justify. It is simply none of your business.' He stepped further away from her.

'I will escort you back to the house,' he said formally. 'The local snakes don't like the gravel of the path, but we are approaching their mating season. They too tend to become a little annoyed if someone interrupts them,' he added, a touch of sly malice punishing her city-bred ignorance.

They returned to the house in silence. Cynthia felt stunned by the result of her stupidity, her body still clamouring for his touch, yet her mind unwilling to intervene.

He opened the front door for her and paused with his hand on the handle. 'I hope you enjoy the rest of your stay. You will forgive me if I take my leave now. I do not expect that we will meet again.'

He had turned away, obviously preparing to leave, when he paused a moment and turned back, a wry grin relaxing his features.

'I have always envied Andrew. Now I understand why,' he said cryptically, and then turned away.

Cynthia watched him in silence as he walked away, around the side of the house and, as he obviously intended, out of her life.

It was some time before she recognised that anger had stripped his speech back to its underlying precision, all traces of an Australian accent lost.

She had no idea how long she stood there, aware of nothing but her bitter disappointment, her mind replaying every exchange, confirming her stupidity. She could no longer remember what it was she had set out to achieve, or why she believed it was possible. She should have trusted her instincts and sent him a dozen bottles of good wine, just to show that she understood the truth and let the matter rest at that. Confronting him had been an aberration that she could no longer justify. She must now escape from an uncomfortable situation of her own making.

In the morning, she found that Drew had made her escape a little easier.

'There are just the two of us for breakfast,' Dulcie explained. 'Drew left early to go back to Mansfield. He's riding in the Cattleman's Cup next week and wants to look at the course again. He sends his apologies for missing you this morning.'

There was a questioning air in Dulcie's manner, but Cynthia chose not to enlighten her, switching to the operation of the B&B

instead. 'I meant it last night when I said how impressed I am with this place. I can't recall seeing anything quite as good. You really have something to be proud of here.'

'The credit belongs to Drew. This is like everything he does. It has to be the best. He spent a year setting it up, doing most of the work himself. Then he brought Jack and I in to operate it. We are the proprietors, but it is owned by the Mitchell Livestock Company.'

Which means that Drew Mitchell owns it, Cynthia thought. The report of the private inquiry agency made a point of his controlling interest in the Mitchell Livestock Company. He paid it all the proceeds of his prospecting. This explained Dulcie's deference last night. Drew might be family, but he was also her boss. One who was conscious enough of his position to avoid a confrontation with Cynthia in front of his staff. It put a different light on so many things. Understanding Drew Mitchell was like peeling an onion; each layer was as baffling as the one before and just as likely to bring tears. She shrugged the thought away and turned her attention to breakfast.

Like the evening meal before, it was superbly prepared, freshly cut fruit salad, chilled juices, farm milk and home baked bread. Staying at Mitchell's Run could make a serious assault on one's waistline.

'I am surprised you are not full all the time,' Cynthia remarked.

'We always close for the fortnight around the Mountain Cattleman's Association Race Meeting. It is our annual family gathering,' Dulcie explained. 'Drew rang from Mansfield to make a special case for your friend. She rang while I was in Omeo shopping and the call diverted to his mobile. He rang me later and asked me to confirm the booking. I assumed he knew her.'

Curiouser and curiouser, Cynthia thought. Nothing was ever as it appeared on the surface in the world of Andrew/Drew Mitchell. She excused herself from the table, packed her things and took a final walk around the lake. It was still very beautiful.

Yet, she did not look back when she drove away, and the noise of the cattle grid under her tires was just an irrelevance.

It was apparent that Drew had manipulated the situation more than she had imagined, not unlike his chess playing in the mine. She had worked it all out, even if she did not know all the details. He had set up their meeting, realising that she was not going to give up easily. It was obvious he had researched her background; the newspaper archives of the society pages would have been a simple source. Her mother's activities and her father's recent Order of Australia had provided enough coverage to give him all the information he needed to recognise Jo's name and connect it to hers. He had even referred to the newspaper photograph of her, and the one that had accompanied the story of her survival had been appalling. No one could have recognised her from that. Not that he had needed it. He had already seen her in the flesh. His surprise at seeing her in the kitchen at Mitchell's Run had been because he was expecting Jo. It was all so simple in retrospect.

What would he expect her to do now? Give up? Persist? Try a new tack? She didn't know . . . and was honest enough to admit that she had little chance of guessing what went on in the complex mind that hid behind the twin masks of Andrew and Drew Mitchell. He sent out so many contradictory signals that picking the truth was, at best, a lottery.

That brought her back to the beginning. What did she want to do?

He was not a man whom it would be safe to love, regardless of the physical attraction that already existed. Like her father, he would follow his own goals, subordinating everything to them. She could never accept that. She had already seen the price her mother paid, and it was not for her.

That did not leave much.

Getting even was not an option. He had saved her life at the risk of compromising his plan to save Mitchell's Run. Having seen the place, she understood why it was important to him, not just the homestead, but the dream of owning the whole valley once more. She could not repay him by putting all that at risk.

That left nothing . . . and her problem was that this was no longer enough.

3

Her invitation to Mansfield for the Mountain Cattleman's Cup came in the post to the South Yarra Boutique on Wednesday morning, two days later. The address was a computer generated label and the invitation professionally printed on stiff card, with a map on the back showing the location of the race meeting and the Mitchell family marquee. Cynthia immediately assumed that someone had mailed it before Drew Mitchell returned to Mansfield. She would have ignored it, had Drew not rung.

'I was less than courteous,' he admitted. 'You caught me by surprise and I over-reacted. I would like to make it up to you.'

'Unfortunately, we have a photo-shoot of our latest collection this weekend. Everything is arranged, the models, the photographer, everything,' she explained regretfully.

There was a pause at the other end, then . . . 'The race meeting might be a good background for a photo-shoot?' He seemed unwilling to take no for an answer.

'Just a minute,' she pleaded. 'I'll discuss it

53

with my partner.'

Jo's response was exuberantly enthusiastic and quite loud.

'I heard that,' Drew admitted when Cynthia returned the telephone to her ear. 'It would seem that you are coming. I shall look forward to it.'

They briefly discussed the requirements for the photo-shoot. Then he ended the call.

Cynthia replaced the telephone hand piece, fumbling a little as she fitted it to the cradle, her mind racing. He had lied to her again. His pride alone made the invitation impossible . . . unless its purpose was important enough to over-ride even that. Which made it very important indeed, and there was only one thing on earth that Drew valued that highly— Mitchell's Run!

Jo ignored her misgivings. She was ecstatic, a bundle of excitement bursting at the seams. She wanted to change everything immediately, ring the models, ring the photographer, add other garments to the photo-shoot, dance Cynthia around the shop. Drew's pride meant nothing to her romantic soul. She was convinced that love conquered all.

'Thank God, one of you has common sense,' she crowed. 'You would have thrown it all away. "We are off to see your hero!' she sang, mangling Judy Garland's song from the Wizard of Oz.

Mansfield is 130 kilometres to the northeast

of Melbourne, about three hours drive through the mountains. It was not far from where the bushranger Ned Kelly and his gang killed the three policemen at Stringybark Creek in 1878, eight years before Andrew Mitchell went missing. It is also the headquarters of the Mountain Cattleman's Association of Victoria.

The Mitchells, strictly speaking, were no longer mountain cattlemen, but they always used the annual Sunday race meeting as a family reunion. Their gathering point this year was to be a marquee set up on the property where they held the race meeting, just outside Mansfield this year. There, they held open house to their guests.

Drew was on the far side of the tent when Cynthia entered. He looked up and saw her immediately, his expression brightened and his lips moved as if he were speaking to himself as he crossed the space between them.

'I am your guest once more,' she said.

'An invited guest this time, and a very welcome one,' he agreed with a smile, which grew when Jo pushed her way past Cynthia and embraced him. Very few men did not smile at Jo. She was petite, vivacious and startlingly pretty.

'I'm Jo,' she said and kissed him on the cheek. 'This is Paul, the photographer; Jenny and Maureen, the models, and all our stuff is in the bus.' The explanation followed the kiss in a single rush of words.

Drew acknowledged the introductions, welcoming each of them warmly. 'There is a parking space at the side of the marquee and a tent set up next to it. We have put in a board floor. There are two tables and I have arranged some poles as hanging space. Let me know if there is anything else that I can do to help.'

This was country hospitality, Cynthia thought, and he does it so well. An outsider would believe that their arrival was a favour to him. He looked the part: cotton moleskin trousers, highly polished R.M.Williams boots, and a light blue Country label shirt with buttoned pockets. He wore the clothes comfortably. This was his natural habitat.

Curiously, her choice of an outfit had matched his almost exactly. She had added a large, brightly patterned scarf, secured with a silver toggle clipped to her shirt by a fine chain and a suede waistcoat with fringed edges. She felt confident. The outfit was appropriate and she knew that it suited her. Her hours in the gym made the fit of the trousers flattering and the shaped shirt emphasised that she was a woman without lapsing into overstatement. Drew seemed to approve. His dark brown eyes warmed almost to a twinkle.

When Jo, the photographer, and the two models returned from the tent, Drew sponsored them as his invited guests. The other major families of mountain cattlemen gathered there accepted them at the same value and they found themselves admitted as equals. In that clannish coterie, it was an impressive tribute to the position of the Mitchell family—and of Drew Mitchell himself.

Cynthia made no mention of her rescue on the mountain, content to bask in the environment that took her at face value. They accepted her initially because they believed her to be Drew Mitchell's friend. After that, it was up to her to provide a reason for that acceptance to become personal.

These Mitchell men gave gifts of value. One of them had given back her life. Another, who might well be the first, now gave her a chance to make a place of her own in his world.

Drew continued his duties as her host, introducing her proudly, including her in his conversations, but she was constantly aware of the photographer and the two girls working in the background. The Mitchell family and their friends were amused enough to cooperate willingly, relieving her concern, so she left the matter in Jo's hands. Jo might have little in the way of business sense but her artistic flair was impeccable. The photographer was an astute professional that they had used before and the girls seemed vivacious and friendly. She had no doubt that they could achieve a satisfactory shoot, but it was important to her that they did nothing to offend their host. His motives might be suspect, but he had gone to considerable lengths to make them welcome.

A burst of activity signalled the first event in the adjacent paddock. Three of the Mitchell men raised the side of the marquee so all could see and Cynthia soon found herself carried along with the crowd, cheering the Mitchell riders and acknowledging the courage and skill of the remainder. It was a happy group. They were comfortable in their loyalties. Winning was secondary. Only the outsiders, who simply knew no better, thought differently.

When the time for the Cattleman's Cup arrived, the atmosphere changed. The serious part of the day had arrived. This is when the mountain cattlemen acknowledged their peers and recognised their best and gamest rider.

The race was a point to point, the exact route determined by the terrain and the rider's courage. It covered a broadly triangular path. The riders had to pass two checkpoints and return to the start/finish line opposite the tent. Other than this, they were free to choose.

The horse Drew Mitchell rode was big and powerful, its eyes alight with a fierce equine intolerance of lesser animals. This was no Timor pony, compact and neat. Instead, it was seventeen hands of untameable power. A coal-black stallion with slashing teeth and hooves to rake any horse or rider that ventured too close, as it stamped impatiently at the start. At best, an uneasy truce existed between horse and rider, more a grudging recognition of opposing strengths than any concession of sovereignty. Yet for all that, Cynthia sensed that they were somehow a matched pair; proud, untameable and game to the point of madness.

'Wow!' Jo said, coming to stand by Cynthia, the photo-shoot abandoned for the moment. 'I can see why you don't want to let this go. He's impressive enough in the flesh, but put him on that horse and he's a god.'

Cynthia bridled, offended by the suggestion that there was anything beyond her need to solve the mystery of her rescuer, though uncomfortably aware that there was.

'He intends to use me,' she defended.

'Big deal,' Jo responded unsympathetically.

The crack of the starter's gun and the roar of the crowd interrupted them. They watched the group of horses stream away towards the nearby hills in a jostling torrent that divided as it passed through the first gate. The steady riders chose the flatter route, skirting the nearest peak. Drew Mitchell led the crack riders and more powerful horses higher across the shoulder, shortening the distance but calling upon the strength of the horses to breast the slope and the broken ground.

Watching through her borrowed binoculars, Cynthia marvelled at Drew's riding. He sat erect in the saddle, legs almost straight, feet thrust firmly into the stirrups. Yet, horse and rider moved as one, each contributing their strength to a determined grasp on the lead, challenging all comers. They crested the ridge, still riding hard, and disappeared beyond. Another distant glimpse, when they topped the farther ridge, was all she saw. After that, the commentary broadcast from the loud speakers was her only guide to the progress of the race.

The appearance of the first flatland riders, augmented by the cracks who had chosen the easier way home, raised a cheer from the crowd.

'Oh God! Will you look at that.' The words burst out of Jo and Cynthia followed the line of her pointing hand to the ridge.

Her gasp of horror was lost, drowned in the roar of the crowd. They too had seen Drew burst over the ridge at full gallop and start down the hill. The slope was steep, rock-bound and cut deeply by erosion gullies, but neither horse nor rider paused in their headlong flight. He was sitting forward in the saddle, his body erect and his eyes scanning the ground ahead. He did not need the spur, the horse was fully committed to the descent and could not have paused without falling. Only the pressure of his knees and the shift of his weight guided the flying animal, for the reins lay loose in his hands. A strange and marvellous alchemy had merged horse and rider into a mythical centaur, clearing fallen trees in its stride and soaring across gullies in a bound. The strike of its iron-shod hooves rang clearly across the distance as the crowd fell silent in fear. If they reached the flats without falling, the race was theirs, but none believed they could do it. One missed step would bring them down and no one believed that either would survive the fall.

Cynthia had no doubt that Andrew Mitchell lived again during that terrible descent. It was the stuff of legend. The Man from Snowy River himself could have done no better! Her own feelings were chaotic. Defining what she felt physically was easier than unravelling the emotional turmoil of fear, elation, terror and ecstasy. Her knuckles ached from the tension of holding the binoculars. Her knees trembled uncontrollably. A Gordian knot had formed in her stomach and her throat muscles tightened to the point where she could hardly breathe as she willed horse and rider to survive.

When they reached the flat unharmed, the crowd vented their relief in a wild roar that seemed to make the ranges themselves tremble. Cynthia had to lean against a tent pole to prevent herself from falling.

'I'm glad it's you,' Jo said, her voice constricted by the tension. 'I don't think I could stand the strain of having him around.'

The ending of the race was an anticlimax, though Drew still covered the final hundred

61

metres at a dead run, emphasising the extent of his victory by scorning the gate and clearing the fence instead. The crowd surged forward and then back in fear as the horse displayed his displeasure at their presence. Foam streaked his chest and flanks while his sides heaved with exhilaration and effort. His nostrils flared angrily at the crowd and he hastened their flight with a barely restrained lunge. His eyes were wild with a burning rage, and his rider was little better, glaring balefully at the fools who hindered their passage to the mounting yard and baulked his horse with repeated roars of applause.

The latter, Drew acknowledged brusquely as the crowd was shepherded clear by the mounted stewards so that he could ride into the railed yard. There he swung down from the saddle and sternly curbed the excited movements of his mount. Walking him around the circuit until his blood had cooled and he no longer lunged savagely at anyone who came near.

Cynthia watched from the rails, her pulse still racing. She had been quite rude, abruptly abandoning Jo to force her way through the crowd. Driven by a compulsion she was afraid to examine too closely, she wanted desperately to catch Drew's attention, to share the moment. He ignored her as thoroughly as he ignored the excited crowd. Lost to them all, still communing with the shade of his ancestor, brought closer by that wild ride.

She left him reluctantly, joining Jo and the Mitchell group to the left of the raised stage carrying the trophies. It would take some time for him to calm the horse and experience had taught her that no woman could compete successfully against a man's perceived duty. Utterly drained, she was thankful for the offer of a seat in the front row. Her feelings sorely tempted her to collapse into it, but she forced herself to sit gracefully, acutely conscious that they had saved the vacant chair at her side for Drew Mitchell.

The minor prize giving was boisterous. Pride and embarrassment seesawed in each recipient, the latter made worse by the loudly spoken comments from their friends in the audience. Drew had rejoined Cynthia. He was again the perfect host, providing a wry commentary, drawing vivid word pictures of individuals and families so that she felt totally involved. His knowledge was impressive and his observations acute to the point of apparent omniscience.

'I can see why you love the mountains,' she said, more than a trifle enviously. 'Your family have made a place for themselves that would be hard to match.'

'It is a long way from what it once was,' he responded regretfully. 'Once, an invitation to Mitchell's Run was in the way of a royal command. As you have seen, the old house is now a B&B and most of the land broken into small packages. The Alpine Park took the rest,' he ended, with a sharp edge of bitterness.

'It's no ordinary B&B and you are steadily buying all the land around it,' she argued.

'Your research is, as always, impressive,' he observed, and she caught the edge of irritation below her host's courtesy.

'I am interested. I owe my life to you . . . or your family. It began as an attempt to pay back a debt. I'm not sure what it is now, but I can't let it go until I have satisfied myself.'

That curious air of detachment resurfaced in Drew. It was as if he had stepped back from the situation to observe and analyse.

'After that . . .' he asked eventually, the pause having grown so long that Cynthia had thought that he was not going to respond at all.

'I don't know. I guess it will depend on what it is that satisfies me.'

'You are a formidable lady, Goldilocks. I can see why Andrew wanted to share his gold with you.'

The whole family spoke of Andrew Mitchell as if he still lived. It fascinated her. A pragmatic lot in every other sense, their generations on the land made them quick to accept reality at its face value, their attitude to Andrew Mitchell was an exception. They accepted him casually as a current fact. If he had walked into the tent right now, he would have created no more stir than any other long absent family member. Either they were all involved in the conspiracy, a real possibility with this family, or Andrew Mitchell was indeed the Ghost of the High Plains!

Cynthia waited in vain for Drew to continue. She expected something—anything, but he seemed content to leave it at that. He was not a man to use words merely to fill a silence.

The presentation for the minor places of the main race interrupted them and Drew seemed to retreat into himself. It was curious that a man who had faced that fearful descent with equanimity was hesitant in the face of a moment's fame.

'Now for the major prize of the day,' the MC began, beckoning Drew forward and lifting the coveted trophy aloft. 'We have grown used to the Mitchell family claiming it, but even Andrew Mitchell would have been proud of the ride we saw today. His namesake has earned this with a flair that would have delighted him.'

Drew came forward, accepted the prize and spoke briefly. He would have retreated into anonymity immediately, but the crowd clapped and cheered repeatedly. They trapped him there, and it was several minutes before they let him go and he could return to Cynthia's side.

Jo broke her unaccustomed silence. The

shoot and the day were finished, she explained. She, the photographer and the two models were ready to go back to Melbourne. Cynthia glanced quickly at Drew. The bus was her transport as well. She could not stay without some intervention on his part and he had yet to reveal his purpose in inviting her here.

He remained silent for so long that she was about to accept defeat.

'We have a dance in one of the wool sheds tonight. My aunt would put you up if you wanted to stay. I doubt that you would find any accommodation in town.'

It was hardly a pressing invitation . . . and she had to rely on only the implication that he would be taking her to the dance, but her spirits lifted sharply. It was the first overt move he had made. She was right in believing in his hidden purpose.

'Thank you. I would like that.'

She tried to ignore Jo's triumphant grin, uncomfortably aware that Drew could not miss it.

'Will you be bringing her back to town . . . or do you want me to come back tomorrow?' Jo asked, never one to leave the lily ungilded.

'You could return tonight if you like. I am sure that Beth would find another bed for you,' Drew said, a smile surfacing as he looked down at Jo's petite form and gamin face. Jo's impish sense of fun was infectious.

'I doubt that my husband would appreciate

it,' Jo responded, still grinning.

'Bring him too. He can sleep in the tent with the rest of the men.'

'Brian's idea of roughing it is to go without central heating in mid summer.'

Drew laughed. 'He would be a trifle out of place then.'

He turned to Cynthia. 'You would honour me by allowing me to escort you home,' he offered, a smile softening the archaic formality.

'Thank you, kind sir,' she responded, with a small curtsy. Jo insisted that Cynthia take a particular dress from the wardrobe of the photographic shoot. She had included it just in case something happened, she said. It was a fine textured wool jersey with a high rounded neckline and a low scooped back. The fit was a trifle snug, emphasising the curves of her body a little more than was entirely comfortable, but the dark umber suited her.

*   *   *

Drew's eyes twinkled wickedly when he called to pick her up from his aunt's home to take her to the dance, his pleasure evident.

'You will turn a few heads tonight,' he predicted.

Something in his voice created an inner glow in Cynthia. It began deep in the pit of her stomach and suffused every part of her body.

She felt suddenly as if she were crackling with energy.

'We'll see you at the dance later,' Beth, Drew's aunt, said, having come to the door with Cynthia. 'Drew knows where the key is kept, just in case we're not up when you get back.'

The motherly air amused Cynthia, particularly as Beth was younger than Drew. An oddity of large extended families, she supposed, yet Beth fussed over him as if he were barely into long trousers and had quizzed Cynthia gently like an overly protective mother.

'Does that mean I can stay out late tonight, Auntie?' Drew asked in a small boy's voice, a warm smile robbing the words of offence.

'He thinks he's Peter Pan,' Beth confided to Cynthia, 'always going out to defend the frontiers of the Mitchell kingdom, always trying to turn back the clock to revive our fortunes. I despair of him ever growing up.'

'Thank you, Auntie,' Drew interrupted, his smile still warm, but the twinkle in his eyes had diminished slightly. 'I will spirit Goldilocks off to Never-Never Land before you start discussing my toilet habits.'

'Andrew has been dead a long time, Drew. It is not your job to bring him back to life. No matter that you're this generation's homage to his memory,' Beth warned, and Cynthia warmed to the first sensible approach to

68

Andrew Mitchell. It showed a family schism on the subject, no matter how lightly Beth expressed it.

They made the short drive to the dance in a comfortable silence. Cynthia felt no need to speak. Everything was going well for a change. She did not want to do anything to challenge that unusual state.

The woolshed was a blaze of lights when they reached it. There were cars and four-wheel-drives parked along either side of the entrance road, but Drew went past them all and parked next to the door itself in a right-hand space held against all comers by one of the Mitchell teenagers. He came around to open the door for her, but a laughing half-dozen of the younger riders, who had been standing on the steps, beat him to it. He stood behind them with one eyebrow raised as she stepped out of the car.

'I did warn you,' he said, extending his hand to escort her into the shed.

Once on the dance floor, Drew proved that his talent as a rider came from a natural sense of rhythm. He danced well, leading firmly without dominating, allowing her to follow his movements naturally without extension. She was acutely conscious of his nearness. The faint masculine tang of aftershave filled her nostrils and the crisply ironed fabric of his shirt pleasured her fingers without concealing the play of the work-hardened muscles beneath. The subtle guidance of his hand in the small of her back sent fingers of fire throughout her body, making it difficult to concentrate on their casual conversation.

Her partner for every dance, except those claimed, with varying degrees of bravado or embarrassment, by the heroes of the day's racing, he had been right about her turning a few heads. Her presence seemed to challenge, or daunt, the younger men according to their character.

'They make me feel terribly old,' she commented, safe in his arms once more after dancing with one particularly bashful young man.

'Positively ancient,' he agreed dryly. 'They will probably never again in their lives be this close to so beautiful and sophisticated a lady. Blaming them for feeling a little daunted is cruel.'

'Do I daunt you as well?'

'A little . . .'

'Why?'

'I chatted to Jo earlier. Your joint venture has met with considerable success, and much of it she credits to your determination and business dealings. My own experience suggests that you are a forceful and determined lady. I cannot imagine anything stopping you. For us lesser mortals, it is all a bit daunting, especially when you wrap it up in such a startlingly beautiful package.'

His considered reply to a piece of light flirtation caught her off-guard and she faltered momentarily in mid step. The gentle pressure of his hand in the small of her back carried her forward and they continued the dance in silence as she considered his words.

She always knew that the perception of beauty was a two edged sword. A lesson she learnt the first time that an opponent had patronised her as decorative rather than functional in a university debating team. She had dealt with it since, not analysing its effect in her own attitude until now. Demanding acceptance as an intellectual equal by the men she met in business, she found they usually granted it, though not without resistance. Drew had just made her question the cost to herself. To daunt a man so self-possessed and self-sufficient was no mean feat!

The music ended and Drew guided her back to the corner of the shed he had subtly claimed as his own. It was a small private place in a crowded room. No one entered it except by his tacit invitation, though she now realised her own personality had some effect in declaring the borders.

'Give us the gift to see ourselves as others see us,' had been Robert Burns' contribution to folk psychology. The gift came infrequently. When it did, it was usually uncomfortable . . . and much easier to ignore, she concluded. It was so much more comfortable to pretend that it never happened.

Peter, Dulcie's son, claimed the next dance. He had come second in the main race. It gave Cynthia the chance to exercise her talents to put him entirely at ease. It was surprisingly easy, just a shift in perception. One she could not believe she had never made before. Her appearance, backed by the Sheldon wealth and her own academic achievements, had created an unconscious assumption that she was somehow born to rule. Drew had just introduced her to the reverse side of that assumption; the obligations that should accompany it—its 'noblesse oblige'—and it felt very good.

'You will create an army of willing slaves,' he complimented her as they began the subsequent dance together. 'I think young Peter would cheerfully die for the chance to serve you.'

'He should do well at agricultural college,' she replied, the warmth of his words making her glow inside. 'It's obvious he loves the land.'

'Unfortunately, that is not enough these days,' he disputed gently. 'We have all hidden in the past too long. The cost of catching up with modern methods is escalating too rapidly and the returns are too uncertain. The future belongs to those who can find the money now and use it effectively.'

'You make a private goldmine sound like an essential agricultural tool,' she said, half joking. 'It seems to have worked very well with you.'

The smile left his face and his eyes hardened as he considered that remark. 'No one could suggest that you are not persistent,' he said coolly. Then he grinned briefly at some private thought triggered by his words and a contemplative smile persisted as they danced. She had the feeling she had just tempted him to some mischief and he was toying with the idea.

The suspense of waiting for him to act and the knowledge that he was deliberately provoking her to some ill-considered action tore at Cynthia. She strove to maintain her composure and keep the conversation casual. He responded with humour so dry that she frequently missed the point for several long seconds after he had spoken. It became a game between them. A mental fencing match with words as foils. The strikes recorded by wry smiles and the warming of two brown eyes.

She always excelled at this type of social repartee and felt herself Drew's equal for the first time since that opening chess game at the mine. It seemed to please him and he acknowledged her successes with a grin. She found herself unreservedly enjoying the company of a man for the first time since her father went to Africa, acutely conscious that a new factor had entered their relationship.

After the last dance, Drew drove her back

to his aunt's home. He thanked her courteously for her company, taking her right hand in his. For a fleeting moment, she expected him to raise it to his lips, but he did not. He merely gave it a chaste handshake and departed for the tent. She watched him stride away, conscious of her own disappointment and of a sudden physical feeling that she had lost yet another game to this man.

A strange bed and an impossible man are not a recipe for sound sleep, nor was the feeling that events were moving beyond her control. She was tired enough, as it had been a long day and she had forgotten how much energy a night of dancing demanded, yet sleep still eluded her. She lay on her side, staring at the slightly paler rectangle of the window, conscious of the country quietness, wondering what she should do.

The day had been Drew's, there was no doubt of that. He had set it up, controlled the pace, and manipulated her feelings. Looking back, it was like the chess games. She could see how each move flowed into the next. How he had adapted her responses to his overall strategy. It was a little frightening in an oddly exciting way. She had never been the focus of so capable a man.

What did he want from her? That was the question.

An affair; her father's money, or was there some darker purpose? In spite of the illegal mine, she could not imagine Drew being less than honourable. It was inherent to his nature. She had the evidence of it in his revelation of 'noblesse oblige'—the responsibility felt only by those who deserve nobility.

That left an affair or her father's money.

The former would be quite pleasant. It would not be her first. The others had been brief, all with Cynthia firmly in control. This one would be different, but the outcome would be the same. She was not yet ready for marriage.

Yet, that was the only path to her father's money with any chance of success, and she would never marry Drew Mitchell. He was too much like her father. The man who became her husband must have no divided loyalties. He would place her before anything. She would not compete with noble purposes, whether they be starving Africans or a rural dream. She was not like her mother!

Her thoughts made it impossible for Cynthia to lie still, making her toss and turn restlessly until she threw back the bed covers and stood up. Two steps took her to the window and she looked up at the blaze of stars, seeking peace in their beauty. She leaned forward until her forehead touched the glass. It felt wonderfully cool, as if the tempo of her thoughts had brought on a fever. She turned her head to bring her cheek against the glass and stood there feeling the chill restore her self control as her thoughts returned to Drew.

The only answer left was an affair, a brief blaze of lovemaking that she could enjoy and then forget. She would pay her debt and put Drew Mitchell behind her, purged of this fever. It felt right.

Tomorrow, she would make it happen.

4

The next morning she was enjoying the sunshine on the northern verandah of Beth's home, drinking tea from a country-sized mug and listening to the end of the ten o'clock news broadcast. Breakfast had been a noisy affair. The house was bulging at the seams with guests, a high proportion of them young and boisterous. Not even Drew had escaped their attention and he had led their retreat to the verandah. He was leaning against one of the verandah posts, sipping his tea and regarding her quizzically. The gentle dry humour of last night had returned with the sun. It added sparkle to what was, in reality, commonplace conversation; confirming the rightness Cynthia had felt by the window last night.

'I would like to go up into the high country and search for the mine. Will you help me,' she asked, speaking quickly, hurrying to get all the words out before Drew could interrupt.

His expression was an unreadable mixture of satisfaction and wariness. She had the feeling that she managed to surprise him by doing what he expected, but in a manner different enough to make him wary. It was so much like a similar moment in the mine that her certainties returned in full strength.

'Is this some form of test?' he asked mildly.

'No. If I am to accept that a ghost rescued me, I must see where it happened,' she explained, carefully not thinking of her ulterior motive. He seemed to be able to read her mind whenever he chose.

'That sounds suspiciously like a baited hook,' he accused, a mobile eyebrow arching to emphasise his question. Her heart stopped at the apparent confirmation of her fear . . . until he continued. 'Are you really saying that looking at some worked-out and deserted mine is going to satisfy you? That you will then accept that a ghost rescued you?' His disbelief was open.

'If I am ever likely to find the mine, you are the one that has the skills to help me,' she explained, deliberately ignoring his scepticism. 'I know of no one else.'

'You've been willing to pay for expert help before,' he responded unhelpfully. 'I've no doubt you could find the resources you need, if you looked for them.'

'I've asked you,' she pointed out earnestly, allowing herself to slip into the slightly pleading pose. 'I'm prepared to pay for your time. Will you help me?'

'Yes,' he agreed, a wry grin completely changing the complexion of the exchange. 'I can see that I shall have no peace until you have satisfied yourself. You can put "Little Orphan Annie" back into her box now,' he instructed. 'You're working her to death. My sisters and female cousins made her all too familiar. When do you want to go?'

'How long will we need to be away?' she asked cautiously, surprised at how quickly he had capitulated, a flush suffusing her face at his instant recognition of her ploy. 'I'll need to make arrangements with Jo.'

'At a pinch, it could be done in two days, but we should take four. We'll drive up and stay at Mitchell's Run overnight. That will give us a full day to ride up to the mine and have a look around. We'll sleep there and ride back the next day. Another night at the homestead and then drive back the following day.'

'You know where the mine is,' she accused sharply.

'Of course. You didn't follow your research far enough. Andrew left a map. However, he had worked out the reef and there was nothing left. Three men went bankrupt during the 1920's proving that there was no gold left.'

'The three that he rescued?'

'Yes. They weren't interested in finding a body. They tried to keep the mine secret, not guessing that it didn't matter.'

'How many people know about the mine?'

'The family, the Department of Natural Resources and Environment. Andrew registered his claim at the time. As many people who chose to inquire. The Vic Parks Ranger Service had to fit doors to the entrances and vents to keep out the hikers. The claim predates the Victorian Parks Act and the grandfather clause would allow it to be worked, if it was profitable.'

She was stunned. He had turned her carefully constructed fantasy into nothing but the absurd romantic daydream he called it at Mitchell's Run.

'Why didn't you explain this in the beginning,' she said. 'It would have saved so much time.'

'You were having too much fun,' he countered. 'Your own ideas had taken charge and nothing could have dissuaded you. Besides that . . .' he grinned mischievously at her. 'I was interested to see how far you would go to prove a point.'

'You expected me to ask you for help to find the mine,' she accused, connecting the hints she had received last night and this morning.

'It seemed probable,' he agreed. 'You're not one to waste time. Proving that you are right is important to you.'

'You are very blunt.'

'Yes.'

He stood there, that superior half smile on his face, challenging her to continue the exchange that his bluntness had made unprofitable. It infuriated her.

'How much will you charge?' she asked, changing tack to impose her own control on the situation.

'Whatever it costs me,' he answered, flanking her attack and maintaining his control.

'Can you give me a ball park figure?'

'Why . . . ? Do you want to haggle?'

No.' She accepted defeat for the moment. 'When?'

'The long-range forecast suggests that the weather will be good from Thursday and through the weekend. I could pick you up Thursday and you would be back home Sunday night.'

'Good.'

She struggled not to give way to tears, studying the mug in her hand quite intently. Anything to avoid his eyes. Every meeting with this man was the same. A roller coaster ride in which sharp-edged confrontation replaced gentle courtship in the blink of an eye, keeping her always off-balance. All she had wanted was to give him more time. The kiss at the homestead proved that he was interested, but her reaction there had made him wary and led to his current teasing approach. She understood what he was doing, so she should have been less vulnerable, but she wasn't. She turned away and looked out at the mountain peaks to the east, certain that her eyes were gleaming with unshed tears.

'Have you time to go for a ride today?' he asked, his voice surprisingly gentle, his experience with sisters and female cousins apparently adequate to the task of recognising her emotional state.

'Yes. I would like that,' she answered, not turning back to face him. His sudden shift in tone had done nothing to reinforce her control. She blinked furiously to hold back the tears.

'I'll make the arrangements,' he said from behind her and she heard the strike of his boots on the wooden verandah as he strode away.

'Thank you,' she said, too belatedly for him to have heard.

She moved a pace to her right and leaned her forehead against the smooth wood of the rounded upright. It was only that she was tired, she told herself, when the tears rolled silently down her cheeks. It had nothing to do with the man who had just left . . . yet the tears continued to trickle down her cheeks unchecked.

'He's the most frustrating man that I know.' Beth's voice startled her. 'I had a terrible crush on him when we were younger. It drove me to distraction until he made us friends instead.

Like everything that he does, it worked; but not enough for me not to envy you a little.'

Cynthia turned and accepted the man's handkerchief from Beth. She dried her eyes carefully, buying time until she could speak normally.

'When he changed his name to Drew, I thought that he'd escaped our curse,' Beth continued. 'He is certainly strong enough . . . yet Andrew rose from the grave and claimed him, none the less. We sacrifice our very best to the memory of that man.'

There was bitterness in the other woman's voice and her expression confirmed that Beth was not one of Andrew Mitchell's fans. The inference was fascinating enough to rescue Cynthia. She could feel the need for tears recede.

'I believe you met our Andrew.' Beth filled the small silence to give Cynthia a little more time. 'What was he like?'

'Too much like Drew to be believed.'

'I can understand that,' Beth agreed. 'Drew is the closest we have ever had to the original.'

Cynthia's mind came to life. Beth was ready to throw open the family closet for some reason. Whatever that was, Cynthia intended to take full advantage of the opportunity.

'How do you know that?' she asked, more to keep the conversation flowing than because she needed it explained.

She could learn many things from Beth, who

82

had lived away from the family while she studied in Europe. It explained both Beth's outside perspective and her detailed knowledge. She had only come back when she had inherited the Mansfield house, bringing her husband, a Canadian grown tired of bitter winters and totally besotted with Australia . . . and his wife. Cynthia had met him last night and had been impressed at how well he fitted into the Mitchell family. It did not explain Beth's willingness to share her knowledge with an outsider. However, while that puzzled her, Cynthia was willing enough to learn from an expert and judge the source later.

Some of the things, she already knew. The succession of Andrew Mitchells was one instance. Others, like the journals Andrew had kept all his life, merely extended her knowledge.

'Were the journals foolscap sized and bound in dark brown leather?' she asked.

'Yes,' Beth confirmed. 'Have you seen them?'

'I think so,' Cynthia said. 'He was writing in one when I woke up the second time.'

Beth had already extracted the story of her rescue, so she merely nodded. 'Probably one of the ones that were lost until recently,' she said.

Cynthia's blank look prompted an explanation that Andrew had given four of his journals to the family lawyer to hold until after his death and these had only turned up recently. The uncertainty of his fate prompted the lawyer to put them aside and they had lain forgotten in his document vault until his descendants cleaned it out several years ago.

'What was it that he wanted to keep hidden?'

'He fought the Zulu in Southern Africa. He was ashamed that he enjoyed both the action and the killing. He must have been an unusual man, particularly for his time. I think he would be horrified to find that we have turned him into a hero straight out of Boy's Own stories.'

'Have you?'

Beth's eyebrow lifted at Cynthia's question. It was obviously a common Mitchell trait; to expect their companions to think before they spoke.

'Every Mitchell child learns his legend as soon as they are old enough to understand. Drew rode Shaka yesterday, named after the most famous Zulu chief. Every Andrew Mitchell has owned such a horse. I think you could say that we have made Andrew our Beau Ideal.'

It was true, Cynthia thought, and Drew Mitchell was the epitome of that ideal. He had modelled himself so completely on his ancestor that he must find it difficult to decide where he stopped and Andrew began. It was very easy for him to impersonate Andrew, he was already halfway there.

'Are you ready to go?'

Drew's voice came from the far end of the verandah. She could see two horses hitched to the fence behind him.

'Yes,' she replied confidently, returning the handkerchief to Beth. She would not need that any more.

They rode away from the house, cutting directly across the home paddocks towards the hills. She wanted to take a closer look at the final hill of the race. To see at her leisure the descent this man had made at such breakneck speed.

'You ride well,' he commented, after they had been riding for fifteen minutes—the first words spoken since they left the house. 'You relax and move with the horse. It's not as tiring for either of you.'

The compliment barely registered and she responded off-handedly, her mind still busy with the new certainty that this had been the man in the mountain mine. She had been a fool not to recognise his manipulation of the events. He had given her plenty of warning. His chess playing had been the same, full of subtle misdirection and sly background manoeuvres. She had his measure now. It would be his turn to dance to her tune!

There was a tiny voice in the far recesses of her mind that whispered heresy. She was overreacting, it said, throwing up the memory of a kiss, the feel of Drew's body as they danced and the outrageous twinkle in his eyes when he had seen her in the dress last night. Cynthia shrugged them off angrily. He had treated her like a fool. She would show him that she was not!

She had two days to check all his statements about the mine. If they were true, there was probably some massive cost penalty to operating a mine in a National Park. That would explain the scheme to avoid it. He was probably planning to show her some other mine in the hope that she would not know the difference. She had some particularly vivid memories of that night. He would not fool her that easily. She now had a lot to do before Thursday.

Impelled by this sudden need for haste, she thudded her heels into the ribs of the smooth-gaited mare she was riding. The startled animal snorted its indignation and leapt forward into a gallop, abandoning the distance-covering lope for a burst of speed up the slope. The horse Drew rode matched the change in pace easily. As a tall man he naturally preferred big, powerful horses, and his chestnut gelding galloped comfortably at the mare's quarter.

She pointedly ignored him. She had trapped herself. Anything she did now would appear foolish. Lacking the courage to allow the horse to return to its natural gait, she drove the willing mare up the slope. At the crest, she would be able to stop without revealing her mistake . . .

She had not reckoned on the mare herself. The drum of male hooves at her rear triggered a reaction that was as old as time itself. The mare stretched herself into a full gallop, driving diagonally across the slope towards the point where Drew had burst over the crest in the race. The gelding responded equally to a vague memory it no longer understood and paced the mare. Out of the corner of her eye, she saw the reins tighten as Drew curbed the gelding. The mare had no interest in getting too far ahead, so this held their speed within the limits of Cynthia's ability.

It was still fast enough to be exhilarating. The thudding tempo of the hooves lifted Cynthia's pulse and her hair streamed behind her in the wind of their passage. Drew had adjusted her stirrups before they left, leaving them long enough that she had unconsciously adopted the riding style he had employed so successfully. She was surprised how comfortable she felt. Trained by an English rider, she was more used to her feet being back rather than forward with knees almost straight. Her scarf tore loose from the silver toggle and floated away behind her, but she did not care. Carried along with the mare's playful spurning of their companions, Cynthia felt all the primeval excitement of the chase.

They reached the crest and the view beyond burst upon Cynthia. This was the last of the foothills and mountain peaks stretched away before her in serried ranks. The sunlight's refraction through the unseen mist of eucalypt oil painted the valleys blue. It was magnificent! Her breath caught in her throat and her heart ached with the sheer beauty of it. She drew rein unconsciously and the mare danced skittishly, still driven by instinct to run.

'Let her walk a bit to cool down,' Drew instructed, as he reached her.

She turned to face him, her heart thudding with the excitement of the ride and her eyes wide with the wonder of the view. It stopped him in his tracks. His mouth opened to issue more instructions as to the care of the mare, but no words came out. It made him look almost comical and she laughed aloud for the joy of it. This seemed the first time that he had reacted normally and she exulted in her power.

'Thank you,' she said, reaching out to take her scarf, which lay, completely forgotten, in his hand. He must have snatched it out of the air as they rode.

'You're welcome,' he responded distractedly, allowing her to take it, his eyes focused wonderingly on her face.

'You are still the most beautiful thing I have ever seen,' he said softly. His voice seemed altered in timbre and so full of gentle wonder, that a part of Cynthia she had never known existed till this moment burst into being and her whole world shifted centre.

'You said that last on a mountain,' she reminded him gently. 'It was snowing, and you were about to leave me.' Her victory had come . . . and was now completely meaningless.

'It was in the marquee yesterday. You had just walked through the entrance,' Drew corrected her, his eyes hardening into coldness.

'What does it matter if I know, Drew,' she reproved him tenderly. 'I'm on your side.' She reached out to reassure him physically.

'This has gone far enough,' he responded harshly. 'The people on my side believe what I say.'

His anger was unmistakable. This was not the cool wariness, nor the dispassionate objectivity he had displayed previously, but the fierce blaze of patience tried too far—allied to an implacable icy will.

She recoiled, snatching back her hand as if he had suddenly become an angry tiger snake poised and ready to strike.

'I have to go up into the hills on Thursday to check on an area that the aerial surveys indicate is prospective. You are welcome to come, and I will detour to show you the mine, but I have heard all that I want to hear about what you believe—or don't believe!'

This was not a man to cross when he was so close to turning back the clock and making Mitchell's Run live again. He obviously saw her persistence as a threat of some form . . .

Cynthia's reaction to Drew Mitchell a few moments before had shattered all her plans. Any affair with him would be like riding the black stallion, Shaka. Wild, exhilarating and far beyond her ability to control. She stared at him almost blindly, her mind battered with half-formed thoughts and crazy, unfulfillable yearnings.

'I'm sorry,' he said, the words coming haltingly as he fought to control his anger. 'That was completely unforgivable. It must be very hard for you to accept. I sometimes forget that not everybody has lived in Andrew Mitchell's shadow all their lives.'

A nod was the only acknowledgment she could trust herself to make. Her own conflict had dimmed her perception of her surroundings. They were the only two people in the world at this moment. The magnificent view had paled and the mare's restive stamping was an irrelevant background noise. She felt as if she were teetering on the brink of a chasm whose depths she could never plumb. It would take only one mistaken step and she would be lost. There would be no turning back. She would never control this man. She was not even sure if the apology had come from the man or the host.

'Drew, I'd like to go back,' she said eventually, when she had mastered herself enough to speak, but she did not look at him. That was a risk beyond her capacity for the moment.

'Very well,' he responded, not questioning the change even in the inflection of his voice. 'If you walk the mare directly down the hill, we can cut through the home paddock and come to the house at the side gate.'

Cynthia looked back over her shoulder at the view. It was still magnificent. She would have to come back and see it again, but not with this man. That would be too dangerous.

The mare picked her way down the slope and Cynthia let her have her head. The horse was mountain bred and could choose a route far better than her rider. They crossed and recrossed the marks of Drew's ride as they descended the slope and it was only gradually that she recognised there were the marks of at least a half dozen descents. Most of the hoof-prints were at least a week old.

'You practised coming down this way?'

'Yes,' he agreed off-handedly.

She glanced back at him, half-fearing to meet his gaze, but he was hardly aware of her. His thoughts were elsewhere as he rode without conscious effort, allowing the gelding to follow meekly in the mare's trail. Cynthia did not pretend to herself that she knew this man well enough to predict his actions, but she recognised his analytical detachment and reminded herself how often he had fooled her. She could take nothing for granted; even his apparent heroism in riding down this slope in the race had turned out to be a carefully practised stunt. Remembering her near terror as he had flown down this slope on Shaka, she felt cheated by the knowledge and furious with herself that she had been so easily swayed into partisanship.

They reached the house without breaking the silence and found one of the younger Mitchells waiting to take the horses.

'Lunch is ready,' the youngster announced, 'Mum said I should look after the horses.' Cynthia dismounted and meekly handed over the reins.

'I'll run you back to Melbourne as soon as we've eaten,' Drew offered, his voice as cool as the weather, now that clouds had covered the sun and reminded her that it was still early spring.

'Thank you,' she said, 'I'll be ready.'

Drew nodded his acknowledgment and strode away in the wake of the horses, leaving her to make her way into the house to pack her few belongings.

The house was still crowded and boisterous, so it was easy for her to avoid being alone with Drew during the meal. She did not know how she was going to cope with the three-hour drive. She really needed more time . . .

He solved the problem for her by filling the car with other guests returning to the city. It gave her shielding company and allowed him to drive in near silence. There were still people in the car when they reached her home in South Yarra's upper class area.

'I'll ring you Wednesday evening,' he said as she stood on the footpath and Cynthia nodded, stepping back from the car to end the conversation. She endured the direct probe of those brown eyes for what seemed an eternity and then he turned away and drove off.

Never had her home seemed so welcoming. She fled the outside world, with its strange baffling men and complex uncontrollable situations. She needed time to think, time to bury the memory of a single moment in time in which she had glimpsed the depth of her mother's pain.

She would never go up into the mountains again with Drew Mitchell. On Wednesday, she would have her excuses ready, and on Thursday, she would begin the task of forgetting that she had ever met him.

The pile of mail stacked neatly on the hall table caught her eye. The housekeeper was very good about this, always clearing the mailbox. Too restless to sit still, she rose from the couch and picked up the bundle of envelopes. Most were business letters, none of them urgent, while the rest were junk mail—except one! It was from the inquiry agency her father had hired to provide the background information on Drew Mitchell and his family.

Cynthia used the ebony letter opener sent from Somalia by her father, to slit the envelope neatly and remove the five pages it contained. The first was a brief covering letter from the agency. It reminded her that they had recommended the analysis of the gold in the nugget for comparison with the analysis of the gold Drew Mitchell had been converting into cash to buy back Mitchell's Run. 'The results must be considered significant,' was the final sentence of the letter. She put this aside and began to read the report. The preamble was boring in the extreme and she skimmed through it, picking up only that the alloying elements in gold deposits varied quite widely and could be used to identify the general location of the find in geological terms. She was not quite sure what that meant, but she read on, completely ignoring two pages of figures. On the final page she found what she was looking for, the results of the analysis and the conclusions that they supported.

'The high purity of the sample suggests a deep reef in an area of considerable geological movement in a median era. The most likely source would be mountainous country and deep mining. This contrasts quite sharply with the analysis sheets provided. These cover low grade ore subjected to simple amalgam processing.'

Cynthia sat stunned. It was impossible. Ghosts simply do not exist! Yet, the difference in the gold quality was so great, there seemed no other answer.

'People on my side believe what I say!'

The words echoed in her mind. Over and over, she heard them. The fierce anger in their delivery burnt indelibly in her memory. What had she done?

The sun disappeared from the sky outside and night fell, yet she remained seated on the lounge, her mind flip-flopping between possibilities. Drew Mitchell was lying. Drew Mitchell was not lying. She could hold onto neither. Without going up into the mountains, she would never know, but to go up to the mountains would be to risk her mother's fate.

The prospect of that lonely life terrified her. For ten years, she had watched her mother play a secondary role to jealous Duty. She had seen her helplessness, caught in an unwinnable war against a cold, pitiless goddess of inhuman beauty, whose very nobility rendered her weaponless. It seemed that any man who had paid court to that cold and heartless zealot was totally incapable of loving a flesh and blood woman. Drew Mitchell was just such a man. A man that any wise woman would shun.

5

When the sun returned, the new day brought little relief.

Cynthia had tossed and turned the whole

night, trapped in a recurring review of each moment she had spent with Drew. There had been no escape. Not even the tried and true method of committing it all to paper had helped. For, at one point, she had tried a detailed analysis, to both capture her memories and exorcise their power, but it had been futile. You do not destroy magic so simply. She had only sharpened her recall of that one moment in which she had both won and lost.

Yet there was perfect logic in her reaction at the time. She had recognised Drew Mitchell's power to hurt her and fled. Nothing could be more sensible; a commonsense solution, even if it was mortally compromised by her vivid memories of his humour, tact and courage. Allied to the sunburst of sheer joy that had flooded her mind when she recognised the meaning of his expression, they made her flight sheer cowardice and left her wanting so much more. Yet the risk terrified her! The alternatives were the sharp-tipped horns of a dilemma guaranteed to destroy her sleep.

'Damn!' she swore, when the toast burnt.

'Damn!' she repeated to herself wearily, when the teapot crashed to the floor and scattered shards of china as it sprayed hot tea across the legs of her new white slacks.

'Damn!'

The word was no longer a curse. It was her defeated recognition of yet another disaster as it greeted the low groan from her car's starter motor. She could have done without a flat battery this morning. Already late, she needed the car to visit the Brunswick factory on the other side of town this afternoon.

The automobile association service man took forever to arrive. At least that is how it seemed to Cynthia. He was courteously efficient and had her on her way in minutes, but this did little to stem her irrational anger. Particularly after he pointed out that she had left the internal light switched on. Over the weekend, it had been enough to flatten the battery. He was short, overweight, fair, and spoke with a broad Australian accent. It would be hard to imagine anyone more different from Drew Mitchell. Yet he managed to prove something that she suspected would be the dominant fact of her life over the next few weeks. He made her think of Drew in a dozen odd little ways. A look, a deft professional movement, an unexpected courtesy, each was sufficient to create instant memories vivid enough to ambush her attention. She found herself having to repeat simple tasks because she had completely lost track of what it was she was doing.

The drive to the shop, which normally took less than ten minutes, was a nightmare. The traffic patterns had changed with the hour and her normal unconscious surety deserted her completely. She was trapped by turning vehicles, glared at by irritable male drivers when she distractedly changed lanes, startled out of a momentary daydream by a blast of car horns when the lights changed and she failed to react immediately. That the sight of a young, fair-haired mother taking a dark-haired little boy into his day-care centre had triggered the daydream disturbed her more than anything else. This was going to be much harder than she thought . . .

She turned into the lane behind their shop and swore feelingly when she found her clearly marked parking space occupied by a strange car. Forced to drive on when a delivery van tooted her impatiently, it took another ten minutes to find an empty space within reasonable distance of the shop; and that was at a two-hour meter.

'Hi,' Jo said, her voice bright with anticipation as Cynthia came in through the front door of the shop.

'There's a car in my parking spot!' Cynthia responded ungraciously.

'We are in a bad way. Aren't we?'

'I haven't slept. The toast burnt. My new white slacks are soaking in the tub to get out the tea stains. The car battery was flat and now I can't use my own parking spot.'

'Drew Mitchell has a lot to answer for,' Jo commented perceptively.

'Is it that obvious?'

'Yes.'

It really was good to have a friend. Cynthia felt the tensions unwind a little and she even managed a crooked smile.

'I'll hide in the back until I'm fit to face the customers,' she said. 'There are a number of accounts I need to check before I go out to the factory.'

'That's a good idea. It's still quiet. I'll get us some tea from next door and you can tell me the whole sorry tale.'

Cynthia went through into the stock room/office at the rear of the shop and sat down at her desk. She made careful note of the expiry time of her parking meter on the scribbling pad and propped the pad where she could not miss seeing it. Her notes from last night, she added to the bulky file on Drew Mitchell and his family. Filing them away would allow her to thrust them from her mind. It was time to focus on business matters and force Drew Mitchell beyond the background of her thoughts. She opened the orders file and was soon lost in crosschecking her forward estimates against the factory orders.

Jo came in with the tea and, recognising the frenetic intensity of Cynthia's concentration, put the tall floral-patterned mug on the side of the desk. Placing the second chair so that she could see into the shop, she sat, sipping her tea silently, as she waited for the inevitable pause.

'It didn't go well?'

Cynthia sighed. That was a mistake. There

was the instant, all too vivid, recollection of Drew using the action as an unspoken commentary on events. The pain the memory brought was almost a bereavement.

'It went far too well,' she admitted.

An interrogative lift of one dark eyebrow was Jo's only comment.

'He is not a man for half measures. There is an intensity in him that terrifies me. I began by thinking that I could prove that he was the man in the mine, thank him for saving me and then leave, but it would not happen that way. If I let my guard down for an instant, he would turn my life upside down in a single moment and think nothing of leaving me to go off on some quixotic quest. The most sensible thing for me to do is to back off and never see him again. He is far too good at hiding things. I am still not sure if it was him in the mine . . . and I doubt that I will ever know. He can turn black into white merely by a look.'

The words poured out in a torrent and Jo was too good a friend to do other than just listen.

'But,' Cynthia continued. 'I am finding it is very hard to do the sensible thing. It really is a lot tougher than I thought it would be—just to step back. He is already under my skin and in my mind. The only thing that I know for sure, is that it will be much harder if I let it go any further. As it is, I know it will get better!'

She paused a moment, thinking about her

100

final statement.

'It must get better . . .' she prayed slowly.

Jo reached out and touched her. There seemed nothing to say, so she said nothing. The two friends sat in silence, sipping their tea and contemplating the vagaries men introduced to women's lives.

The photographer arrived ten minutes later. He had a large folder with selected enlargements of the shots he thought best and the three of them sat in a circle as he handed them first to Jo, who then passed them on to Cynthia. As advertising material, they were quite superb. The models were among real people and it showed—the very naturalness of the others serving to highlight the quality of the designs and the effectiveness of the cut.

'I think that we should blow these up and use them as a background for the display in the front window,' Jo said, selecting three of the photographs and passing them to Cynthia.

She used the distraction to slip a half-dozen prints from the folder to the ground with the discards. The move was so smooth that Cynthia noticed it only because of the startled look on the photographer's face.

'Perhaps I'd better see these first,' she said, bending down to retrieve the prints Jo had discarded.

'I don't think you want to,' Jo warned.

'I can be the judge of that,' Cynthia said stubbornly, examining the prints.

All of them featured Drew. The first was a freakish action shot of him coming down the mountain on Shaka. The focal depth of the telephoto lens had compressed the distances so that the distant mountains seemed immediately behind the crest above him. It had frozen horse and man in the moment of landing from a leap across a gully, iron-shod front hooves striking visible sparks from the rock and the man just settling back into the saddle. The horse glared fiercely from the print and it contrasted oddly with the sheer exaltation of the rider's expression.

The photographer beamed proudly as Cynthia admired his work. He was quite prepared to accept the credit for something that had been almost an accident.

Cynthia laid the photograph aside reluctantly and turned to the next. Her sharp intake of breath justified Jo's attempt to hide these prints. The photograph captured Drew in an unguarded moment after the prize giving. He was looking at Cynthia, who was also in the photo, but turned away from him, towards the camera. Something had just caught her attention, for there was an expression of alert interest on her face. The expression on Drew's face was the surprise. It tore a hole in all the defences she had constructed so laboriously.

His lips curved in a slightly wry smile while his eyes held that curious mixture of gentle wonder and pride that had shattered her composure on the mountain ride . . . twenty-four hours after this photograph. Her fingers unconsciously stroked the surface of the print, feeling not the smooth photographic paper, but a crisply ironed cotton shirt and a hard-muscled body beneath.

'I think that we'll look at these and then get back to you later today,' Jo said diplomatically, shepherding the photographer out into the store and leaving Cynthia alone with the remaining prints.

Cynthia was hardly aware of them leaving. She was lost. Only the photographs in her hands had any reality. Drew was in all of them. Mostly with her as well, but in two of them he was on his own. In the second of these, he was accepting the prize for the race, and it captured exactly his reluctance in the face of the fulsome praise heaped upon him by the MC. She was not sure when she started to cry. The tears suddenly appeared on the prints and she had to wipe them dry, her fingers lingering whenever they touched Drew's image. She kept coming back to the photograph of Drew looking at her. It recaptured that moment on the mountain so faithfully—the moment when she had recognised the depth of her peril.

'This was not a good idea,' Jo remonstrated gently, standing beside Cynthia and resting her hand on her shoulder.

Cynthia turned and buried her face in her

friend's embrace. Drew Mitchell was too dangerous and it was all her fault. She had realised the risk from the beginning, yet she had gone on. She could not blame Jo and her father. They had pushed, but she had secretly wanted to go on. The fault remained hers. She should have called a halt after Mitchell's Run. There was no excuse for going to Mansfield . . . the staccato thoughts ricocheted around inside her head until the tears turned into sobs of despair and she lost herself in them. Jo's arms around her were the only reality while her body shook uncontrollably until she exhausted herself.

It was fortunate that no one came into the shop in the next half hour, for it took that long for Cynthia to recover.

'This is ridiculous. I can't go on like this,' she said, disengaging herself from Jo's arms and standing up. 'Put these damn things away somewhere,' she thrust the photographs at Jo. 'I'll look at them later. When I'm not so tired that I see things that cannot possibly be there.' She turned away and walked into the small wash room at the very rear of the storage space.

When she emerged fifteen minutes later, she was outwardly herself again and returned calmly to her work at the desk. She pointedly ignored the folder of photographs at her elbow.

Another mistake! The scribbling block with

104

the expiry time of her parking meter was half hidden behind it.

It was 11.45 before she remembered it. The meter had now been expired for over twenty minutes. She hurried out of the shop, hoping desperately for some of the luck that had apparently deserted her, but the windscreen had a fold of coloured paper under the wiper. Too dispirited to swear, she tore it free and thrust it into her pocket without looking at it. It could wait until the end of the week. She would deal with it then. The world might just be a little brighter. She must move the car if she did not want another ticket—a lesson she had already learnt the hard way.

Her parking space was vacant when she reached the lane. It was a little late, but she was ready to accept whatever favours came her way. There seemed few enough of them.

She and Jo ate a leisurely lunch. It was early in the week and the shop was quiet, so they sat in the sun at the street tables of the adjacent cafe. They would choose who attended any customer who wandered into the shop by a single game of scissors/paper/rock. It was a settled routine. Drew Mitchell was pointedly not a subject of their conversation.

'I'd like that cup of coffee now.'

The voice startled both of them. It came from directly behind them, seemingly emanating from a passing car. It was only when the parking inspector straightened from marking the rear tyre that they saw him.

'You haven't read it yet, have you?' he said, correctly interpreting their bafflement.

'No,' Cynthia admitted guiltily, quickly thrusting her hand into her pocket and retrieving the coloured paper.

'I recognised the car. You owe me a cup of coffee,' was scrawled across the face of an advertising pamphlet for their shop. One that had been made deliberately the colour of a parking ticket, almost two years ago. It had been one of Jo's ideas for publicity before Cynthia had formed the partnership.

'Thank you,' she said gratefully. 'It has been a bad day till now.'

'I've been waiting to get back at you two. You have no idea the trouble that bright idea of yours caused me.'

Les Bowman was in his late forties. He was the human face of the parking inspectors in the area. He would feed a few coins into a meter, or make the official copy illegible for locals. As straight as a die, his actions viewed with a Nelsonian blind eye by all but the thickest town hall official, he remained a local institution. At Christmas, the panniers of his motorcycle bulged with presents from grateful shop-owners and residents. It was an unsolicited vote of thanks for his common sense approach.

He sat with them for twenty minutes, well pleased with himself at having paid them back for the misguided advertising campaign. His coffee, croissant and vanilla slice appeared, as if by magic. It was also oddly absent from their account at the end of the meal. Cynthia imagined that it was many years since he had last paid for anything in that area.

Her world was a little brighter when she returned to the accounts. She felt that she could have even looked once more at the photographs and have been unmoved by them. She did not test this belief. There were times when it was not wise to examine small victories too closely.

The visit to the Brunswick factory went smoothly. The day had now definitely turned for the better. They would make all the scheduled deliveries. It would be a real test of her estimates. If she had predicted correctly, then Jocyn Pty Ltd was in for a third successful season.

Her parking spot was unoccupied still on her return and she swung the small saloon expertly to back neatly into it. She intended an early night tonight. It was time she caught up on things—sleep included. She unlocked the back door to the store and entered quietly. Seated at her desk was a familiar figure . . .

He had obviously been there for some time. Spread out before him on the desk were the photographs and the contents of the file of information she had accumulated on the Mitchell family, including her handwritten notes from last night.

'Hello, Goldilocks,' he said, not bothering to turn around.

White-hot anger shook Cynthia. How dare he, she thought? There was nothing in their relationship that gave him the right to read her personal files. Yet it was so typical of the man that he thought he could. He would never change . . .

He turned to face her and her anger fled. In the time since she had last seen him, her father had become old! The leonine mane was now more grey than blonde. He had lost weight and the mahogany skin of his face had sagged, giving him the beginnings of dewlaps beneath his chin. He was no longer the blonde knight in shining armour whose presence, or absence, had been the major factor in her life. She had to bite her lip to stop herself crying out in dismay.

'Hullo, Dad,' she said simply, crossing the room to embrace him as he came to his feet to meet her.

'I like the name,' he said. 'Goldilocks suits you. He is quite perceptive.' He tapped Drew's image in the photograph.

'How long have you been home?' she asked; Drew Mitchell driven from the forefront of her mind by her concern.

'I flew in Sunday. You should check your answering machine occasionally.'

'I was away Sunday and a bit distracted last

108

night,' she admitted.

'I can see why,' he agreed. 'You realise, of course, that he is the man from the mine?'

'I'm not sure any more.'

'Has he actually denied being the man?'

'N-No,' she admitted uncertainly, searching her memory for Drew's exact responses and finding very few, none of them direct denials.

'Then, until he does, you can assume that he is the man.'

'What makes you so sure? There's evidence that he is not.'

She explained about the analysis of the gold samples, emphasising the difference. Her father had been a very successful executive before taking up the aid agency. Her respect for his judgement remained undiminished by the difference in their personal views.

'He is still the one. I don't know exactly how he did it, but he is far too smart for you to catch him that easily. I would like to see that report. You probably didn't ask the right questions.'

She smiled at her father's staccato certainties. He might look older, but it had not affected the belief that he knew best. A few days together and they would be fighting again. It was almost a relief, after the shock of his appearance.

Until the agency had taken over his life, they had been very close. Even Cynthia's demands for independence in her late teens had not diminished their relationship, but the agency was another matter. She could not believe that so level headed a man as Edward Sheldon could shut out everything, including his family, in the pursuit of a single goal; especially the man who had preached 'balance in all things'. When she had returned the favour the last time he was home, suggesting a reduction of his commitment to the agency, he had looked at her in silence for a long moment. Then he had merely shaken his head negatively, leaving her to guess what he meant.

Jo came in with three mugs of cappuccino and a plate of cakes from next door. She ignored the flash of Cynthia's eyes, aware that she was responsible for Edward Sheldon's access to the files and photographs. He and Jo had always been natural allies. She had never completely agreed that he was at fault in spending so much time away.

He caught the interplay between the two friends and smiled.

'She was worried about you,' he explained unnecessarily.

'I can look after myself.'

'I guess we'll find out about that.'

'What do you mean?' she demanded suspiciously.

'Your mother is having one of her formal dinners tomorrow night. I came round specifically to invite Jo and Brian.' He smiled at her. 'You are invited as well, of course.'

'How many are coming? Is it one of Mother's bigger affairs?'

'Only twenty,' her father said indulgently. 'Quite intimate, really.'

He had never been a willing participant in the social set. It was one of the few things father and daughter had always agreed upon. It was her mother's background, however, so they both endured it for her sake; and it had paid dividends for the shop in recent years.

'I suppose it is the usual crowd?'

'Yes,' her father agreed. 'However, I imagine Drew Mitchell will make it a bit more interesting . . .'

'Dad! You haven't . . . ?'

'He was a bit unwilling at first. That changed when he understood that the invitation was from you. Those photographs make it obvious that the man is already half in love with you,' her father explained calmly.

'I wish you would learn to mind your own damn business,' she said, fighting down an odd surge of elation as she acknowledged her father's judgement.

'It is my business, girlie. I want to meet this man and I do not have the time to stand on ceremony. I fly back on Sunday.'

'You'll never change, will you? When are you going to let me grow up?'

'You are already grown. This is for me, not for you. Just humour me.'

There was something in his tone that caught

111

her attention. It was as close to a plea as he was capable. He was keeping something from her . . .

'Does Drew know just how formal Mother's dinners are?' she asked, signalling her surrender.

'Yes. I warned him that it was a black tie affair.'

6

Exhaustion claimed Cynthia that night and she slept like the dead, waking refreshed and feeling almost confident. A feeling that diminished during the day, eroded each time a reminder of Drew Mitchell ambushed her attention.

Jo had not helped. Having now met Drew and been captivated by him, she considered Cynthia's fears pointless. 'You wouldn't know what to do with someone spineless enough to have no goal of his own,' she argued. 'Drew Mitchell is alive. Be grateful. It is utterly irrelevant whether he rescued you or not. The only fact is that he is interested in you. Grab him with both hands before he gets away.'

Cynthia shook her head at Jo's certainty. It was all right for her to give advice. Brian, her husband, was a stockbroker steadily climbing the ladder of a prestigious firm and totally devoted to Jo. She wrapped him around her little finger as a matter of course and he gloried in it. Drew Mitchell had already proven himself unwrappable.

Cynthia had survived the usual number of high school crushes by the simple expedient of outgrowing them. At the time, they had been unbearable, but, in retrospect, they now seemed very simple and uncomplicated.

The forefront of her mind understood this and the danger that Drew Mitchell represented. It had analysed the situation and decided that it was unacceptable, that she should disengage immediately from further contact. There was, however, a subversive element hidden elsewhere that owed a great kinship to those schoolgirl infatuations, and was no more controllable now than it had been then.

It used all the old weapons: the formless excitement; the breathless anticipation; and the absolute belief that this was a moment like no other before it. There was no aid in logic, nor refuge in decision. It ignored them both, producing wild mood swings that she could neither control nor anticipate. At one moment, she would be a modern young woman, totally in control of herself and her destiny. At the next, she would be an infatuated adolescent at the mercy of her hormones. It was all very strange.

By six p.m., when Cynthia arrived at her

parents' home in street clothes, she felt exhausted once more; yet, at the same time, filled with a restless energy that demanded release.

She dressed for dinner in her old bedroom. It was upstairs at the rear of the house and her mother maintained it immaculately in her absence. It always gave her an odd feeling to walk into the room she had left four years ago and find it so unchanged. So many things had happened to her that it seemed unreal to return to an area unaffected by the passage of time. When she had dressed and put the final touches to her make-up, she stood for a while at the tall windows, looking down at the ornamental garden below, filled with an odd mixture of dread and excitement. Drew would be here shortly and she still had no idea how she could cope with the impossible situation her father had created. Fortunately, her father's return had put paid to any trip into the mountains for the moment. She had a breathing space in that, if nothing else.

Cynthia glanced at her watch for the hundredth time, decided that it was time and turned away from the window, unconsciously squaring her shoulders as she left the room.

The Sheldon house was one of the 'old homes' in the area. It had been built in the era of gracious living that had followed the Victorian gold rush, when the young colony was flush with easily won wealth and aping the old world uncritically. The house had avoided the worst excesses, but the reception area, just inside the front door, was the exception. It was two stories high, had a domed glass roof and featured a vast expanse of terrazzo tiling, complete with marble statues and luxuriant potted plants. Two broad marble staircases curved around the far wall to the upper floor, framing the imposing entrance to the dining room. When she was a child, the area had been her wonderland, and the envy of her friends.

Cynthia had just reached the head of the stairs, a large statue of Aphrodite hiding her from view, when Drew came in the front door. She halted and watched him unobserved, as her mother greeted him.

Jeanette Sheldon was especially gracious. Drew had won her immediate support by sending a formal acceptance of the invitation by courier. The addition of a single, perfect red rose had been an astute master touch. Now he increased his status even further by arriving precisely on the 7.30 chimes of the grandfather clock. Punctuality by a guest was another certain road to her mother's favour.

It was further proof of Cynthia's belief that Drew had researched her family in the society pages before her arrival at Mitchell's Run. The moves were all too perfect to be an accident. Drew Mitchell obviously left little to chance when he was determined to make an impression.

His dinner jacket was not new, but impeccably cut by a master tailor; it would never look old. She guessed that he had visited Savile Row during his studies in England. He had that perfectly tailored look that seemed to come from no other location. He looked comfortable and supremely self-confident, as if he could assume command of the entire room at a whim. The single-breasted jacket opened slightly as he turned to answer a question from her father and it revealed a silken cummerbund of deep burgundy. Startled, she looked down at her dress. They could have cut them from the same bolt of cloth. The colour matched exactly. This was the second time that their choice of colour had coincided. It felt just a little uncanny.

It was now time for her to join them. She moved to her left and started down the sweep of the staircase so that she would come into his direct line of sight. The nervous energy she had expended on every detail of her appearance demanded that she make an entrance. The movement caught his eye and he looked up. A single sweep of his eyes catalogued every detail of her appearance before focusing on her face with an intensity that seemed to make the room pause. She braved his inspection with all the grace she could muster, allowing her lips to curve into a welcoming smile. He nodded slowly in acknowledgment and returned the smile, his eyes mischievous.

It was an outwardly innocuous exchange, something that would have passed without comment in any gathering, but she felt as if a charged field had reached out and gently strummed a resonating chord deep in her soul. He turned away casually in response to a comment from her father, but she knew that the movement was a lie, that he was acutely aware of her. He had come because he believed that she had specifically asked that he be there. Her father was right. The moment caught by the photographer had been the truth. She did not know how it had happened, or what she had done to deserve it, but she had somehow penetrated Drew Mitchell's armour. He was vulnerable. She damned her father for what he had done. It would have been better her way . . . yet that tiny voice in the far recesses of her mind exulted in the knowledge of her power.

Her father beamed at her and Jeanette Sheldon rewarded her with a slow approving nod. The halter-necked dress, one of Jo's designs, had a soft peaked collar, a crossover front that continued into a slim full-length wraparound skirt. This allowed the skirt to open on her right side as she walked. The resulting peep show of her leg, almost to mid-thigh, reached out and snared Drew's attention as she had descended the stair.

'Hello,' he said quietly, the warmth in his eyes making any other greeting superfluous.

'It seems that it is now my turn to be host,' she said, a trifle mischievously. She would show him that two could play word games.

'I was made an offer that I couldn't refuse,' he responded truthfully.

The simple sincerity in those words made her attempt at word games feel cheap. She glanced at her father's face. Surely, he could see how badly he had meddled.

That was all that it took. She had forgotten the razor-edged perception of her guest. He had not missed the glance. The shadow of a question flitted briefly across his face, then was gone. He turned and responded to a question from her mother without a pause, but Cynthia sensed part of his attention was elsewhere. When he turned back to her, the warmth had gone from his eyes. He knew!

He glanced briefly at her father and then looked straight at her, his right eyebrow lifted slightly. She nodded her confirmation, all the movements slight enough to pass unremarked by anyone else. He smiled compassionately and she admired him more at that moment than at any other. She did not doubt his disappointment, but he chose to empathise with her position. Her intellectual resolution to end this association wavered. This man was anything but ordinary.

She was glad when the chiming of the

grandfather clock signalled the move from the reception area into the dining room. 'Dinner at Eight' was no cliché when Jeanette Sheldon entertained. The guests disposed themselves around the long oval table, falling automatically into a male/female sequence from Edward Sheldon's chair. Jo and Cynthia sat to the left and right of him, with Brian and Drew extending the sequence until two males flanked Jeanette at the far end.

Drew's expressive right eyebrow twitched marginally at the smoothness of the seating arrangements.

'Yes,' her father agreed with the implied criticism. 'We are a well-trained lot when it comes to entertaining.'

She could see Drew absorbing the implications rather than the words.

'You don't entirely approve . . . ?' he asked.

'No. Do you . . . ?' her father's eyebrow mimicked Drew's

'I suppose I do. They did it very well.'

'Then a perfect crime would also meet with your approval?'

'Define "crime"?'

'The dictionary would define it as "An offence punishable by law",' she interposed.

'Would that be true if the crime were perfect?' Drew asked innocently, a wicked twinkle in his eyes. The larrikin was never far from the surface with him. 'The obvious proviso of that dictionary definition is "if proven guilty". I believe perfection in this sense should extend beyond mere avoidance of a guilty verdict. The "perfect crime" should exclude the knowledge that a crime has been committed.'

'That's pure sophistry—playing with words,' she accused, smiling.

'Yes,' he agreed blandly, his eyes amused.

Her father chuckled at the exchange, drawing Drew's attention and the two men exchanged smiles.

The lack of antagonism between the two men fascinated her. Drew apparently held no grudge over her father's interference and contributed to the search for common ground, something on which to base an alliance. It was as if they had an agreed private agenda to become friends.

The soup arrived and conversation lapsed into idle dinner table chatter. Cynthia sipped slowly, conscious that both men were observing her minutely. Drew was the less obvious, but she could sense his scrutiny quite acutely. She battled an insane desire to commit some social gaffe, like slurping her soup, just to shock them.

Behind her father, taking up most of the wall above the mantle, was an oil painting of a bush glade by Ern Trembath. He was a local artist with a well-earned reputation for sympathetically capturing the Australian bush and this was one of the best of his early works.

It was her favourite painting and she was pleased to see Drew admiring it.

'It is very good, isn't it?'

'Yes,' he agreed. 'It is one of his early works. He developed a surer touch with water surfaces as time went on.'

She turned to consider the painting. It was amazing. Drew had put his finger on the detail that had jarred at a near subconscious level. The surface of the water lying in the low areas of the glade was not quite right, but she would not have identified the fault without him pointing it out.

'You know your art,' her father admitted, having turned to study the painting himself.

'I admire his work,' Drew agreed, his eyes still studying the painting with an odd sense of longing.

'Do you paint?' she asked.

'A little . . .' he turned to her and grinned in self deprecation. 'Though I have heard people suggest that it is closer to drafting,' he explained.

'I suspect that it is better than that,' she accused.

'You've been to Africa?' her father interjected smoothly, taking advantage of Drew's pause for thought to pursue his own ends.

'Yes. I spent some time there on the way back from the UK. It is still the best place to learn the practicalities of gold mining.'

She only half listened to the resulting conversation between the two men, though Jo, Brian, and the woman sitting on the other side of Drew seemed to find it quite enthralling. It was enough to sit back in her chair and observe her guest. The attention of the others had distracted him enough to allow her an unusual freedom from his awareness. She felt safe for the moment.

The special temporary staff had removed the empty soup plates and there would be an intentional pause before the next course. It was her mother's idea to encourage guests to talk. In good weather, they often strolled in the ornamental garden outside the glass doors that formed the rear wall of the dining room. The special lighting, fountains and small footbridges made it a popular retreat from the dinner table. The garden was now invisible in the darkness; the lighting switched off, making Cynthia regret the chill of the evening. Strolling in the garden would have given them both a break.

Drew was handling the situation impeccably, allowing nothing of his disappointment to show, acting the role of a perfect guest, but there were occasional hints of strain in his manner, visible only because her admiration made her especially responsive. She watched his lips curve into a smile at some comment from Jo and remembered their gentle joining with hers as he had farewelled her in the falling snow above the Chalet, and again at Mitchell's Run.

She paused. This was ridiculous. She was grateful for his recognition of the situation, but nothing had really changed. Drew Mitchell was still too risky a proposition to venture and tonight would see the end of him . . .

'A penny for them.'

Drew was looking at her with a quizzical lift of that damned right eyebrow.

'Secret women's thoughts,' she said truthfully.

'Is having secret women's thoughts politically correct in this day and age?' he challenged, riposting her defence with a grin.

'When did you become a defender of political correctness?'

'Whenever it suits me.'

'Then I can lapse into political incorrectness whenever it suits me,' she reasoned and they both laughed at the indefensible logic.

The words were just an excuse to cover the touch of their minds. Cynthia could feel her resolution fraying rapidly at the edges. It was easy to decide that discretion was the wisest course when a dozen reasons to ignore it did not assault her defences. When her ears could not hear the rich timbre of his voice. When her hand did not tremble with the urge to straighten an unruly lock of hair at his right temple. When a subtle masculine aroma did not hover on the edge of her perception.

When wisdom appeared something better than arrant cowardice.

More as a distraction than anything else, she picked up her wineglass by the stem, sampled the aroma, and held it against the light to admire the colour. She then took a sip, holding it in her mouth for a moment to appreciate the taste before she swallowed. It was an overly pretentious display that she became aware of only when she turned back to him.

The skin around his eyes wrinkled as he grinned at her, but this was poor concealment for the very special caress in his eyes. A tremor ran down her spine to blast an aching void in the centre of her being; one that she already suspected only Drew Mitchell could ever fill. She had to discipline herself into stillness until she regained control.

Fortunately, her father spoke and, having gained Drew's attention, continued his wooing of the younger man. He could charm the fish out of the ocean and it was apparent that he wanted something from Drew. A twinge of jealousy at how intimately the men spoke caught her by surprise. Realms of private information flowed between them in two entirely separate levels of conversation. On the surface, they included everyone at the table. Yet, beneath the surface, was a flow that depended entirely upon common experience— a subtle play of nuances. Couples, long married and comfortable with their lot, achieve something similar.

Her thoughts wandered as she lost herself in an impossible daydream of reaching that status with Drew . . .

'Wo,' Drew used the Zulu expression of amazement as her father switched from English to Zulu in mid sentence. She recognised the word from one of her father's funny stories of the camps.

Her father responded in what appeared to be a different language and the two men played a game of switching languages and dialects in succession. ,

'Bayete!' her father returned to Zulu to salute Drew's achievement. 'You seem to have forgotten very little. To my ear, your accent is good. You could probably work without an interpreter at all.'

A brief frown crossed Drew's face, intriguing her. It was as if her father had committed a breach of Zulu etiquette. Then realisation flooded her mind and all of her father's moves became transparent. He had read the range of Drew's achievements in the file and recognised his usefulness to the agency. A man like Drew would be invaluable in the refugee camps. He had the language skills to communicate and the engineering skills to create drainage, provide water, dispose of waste. Damn him, she thought, glaring at her father. How dare he use her so shamelessly!

'What is your next step in re-establishing Mitchell's Run?' she interrupted, intent on reminding her father that Drew had other commitments.

That damnable eyebrow of Drew's lifted fractionally once more. He did not have to be that acute. Nor did he have to let her see his response. He was actually teasing her with it—relying on the sharpness of her perception to play a little game. It was not fair! He could disarm her by sincerity, making her attempt at word games seem cheap, but still feel free to play havoc with her emotions. It was typically male!

Her father was no better. Two pairs of male eyes regarded her all too knowingly. It was a sharp reminder that she could take neither man lightly. She would have to be subtle.

'You didn't answer her question about Mitchell's Run,' her father challenged, his expression intentionally bland.

Drew matched his expression. 'No,' he agreed.

The silence stretched out and took on a meaning. 'And you don't intend to . . .' her father confirmed verbally.

Drew just smiled at him. No other answer required.

Cynthia blessed her guest's perceptive nature. He had read her father's purpose long before she had. His research before responding to the invitation was once more obvious. This man rarely allowed anyone to see all his cards at the same time. The thought was a little frightening . . .

The two men seemed unaffected by the revelation of Edward Sheldon's purpose, continuing their conversation as if nothing had happened. Her father spoke more openly of his role in the agency, though it did trigger a moment that puzzled her. She did not catch her father's exact words, she was listening to Jo at the time, but they made Drew look down the table at her mother.

He studied her face for a long moment, something close to compassion in his expression, before turning back to her father and nodding agreement. Her father returned the nod and changed the subject, leaving Cynthia wondering what her father had said about her mother's seating arrangements and why they should make him feel guilty.

The dinner went on through its courses and the conversation became light and social. Drew responded knowledgeably on a dozen topics that she would have thought held no interest to him. One of the other guests, a theatre critic with a penchant for demonstrating his erudition, quoted one of Shakespeare's sonnets. Drew not only completed the quote, but also identified the sonnet by number. An accomplished performance that touched a part of Cynthia that she thought beyond the reach of any man. Her throat tightened and she drew a sharp breath that was almost a sob. She reminded herself again not to take this man too lightly. Her emotional reaction to his presence made it easy to lose sight of the reasons she feared an involvement. He had single-mindedly achieved the almost impossible feat of resurrecting Mitchell's Run and would allow nothing to divert him from that purpose. It almost gave her pause—and may even have forestalled her need for him had not the moment arrived for them to move into the next room for coffee and liqueurs.

Drew rose before her and drew back her chair as she came to her feet. Taking his arm as they walked seemed natural, as did the gentle pressure of his other hand as it came to rest on top of hers, yet the effect could hardly have been greater.

It was as if he had thrown a switch somewhere in the control centre of her brain. Her physical sensitivity sharpened to the point where it hovered on the edge of pain. She was exquisitely aware of everything, both around and within. The room lights had become startlingly bright and her every breath seemed to roar in her ears. Every nerve end on her skin clamoured for attention and she could actually feel the lace edging of her bra on the curve of her breast. The gentle friction of the individual fibres of fabric on her skin was so intimate that it became a deliberate caress.

Nothing remotely like this had ever happened before. What it would be like to have this man make love with her she could only guess. She felt a little dizzy at the thought. What had once been a tiny voice from the far recesses of her brain was now trumpeting triumphantly the absolute necessity of finding out. It would be something so far beyond her experience that nothing existed in her past to be her guide.

Her eyes sought his, willing them to respond, to turn away from the others in the room and look at her. They did . . . and their expression completed Cynthia's capitulation. No man had ever looked at her with such power. The way that this evening would end was now beyond conjecture. They needed no words. There was now a pact. She could feel her impatience building . . .

The evening still flowed effortlessly around them, following her mother's carefully structured plan. The staff served the coffee, liqueurs and cheeses in the room that led back to the reception area. The meal itself had spanned three hours and this was the penultimate stage. The guests would move from this room back into the reception area, retrieve their coats and be on their way with a minimum of fuss.

Drew was quietly enjoying it. He had spoken the truth when he had admired the smoothness of the seating routine. Anything done well had his support.

There was something else as well. Cynthia found him looking at her mother once more with that expression of compassion. He hid his thoughts when Jeanette Sheldon approached, a subtle signal that it was his turn to depart. He replaced the compassion with a twinkle in his eye that roused a reaction even in that sophisticated mind. Her smile dazzled as she took his arm and led him away to make his goodbyes.

Cynthia watched him speaking with the other guests, easily drawing smiles and further invitations, then turned away and was face to face with her father. His smug, self-satisfied expression showed that he thought that he had won, that he could use their relationship to his own ends. Her sudden rage took her by surprise.

'What you have done is unforgivable. You deliberately used me as bait to recruit him for your damned work. You will not have him! I'll see to that . . . just as I will have proof that it was him in the mine!'

Cynthia's eyes were fixed on her father's face, her voice low, but vehement. Her determination to wipe the smile from his face made her add the final argument, though, in truth, it was the furthest thing from her mind at that moment. The sharp shift of his eyes to a point beyond her shoulder did not register at first . . . then it did, and she turned sharply.

Oddly, the shock on her mother's face registered first. There could be no doubt that she had heard, nor that she was appalled at her daughter's social gaffe. Cynthia found it hard to shift her eyes to Drew's face. She dreaded what she would see there.

When she did, it was a total stranger who returned her gaze; his expression so completely closed that four lines of one of Shakespeare's more obscure sonnets came immediately to mind.

'They rightly do inherit heaven's graces,
And husband nature's riches from expense,
Who are the lords and owners of their faces,
Others, but stewards of their excellence.'

'It is a pity that we will have to postpone the trip to Mitchell's Run,' he said, rescuing her from the uncomfortable silence. 'I have managed to borrow a friend's plane. There's a bush strip below the homestead.'

The total irrelevance of his words struck her dumb. She just stared at him.

'You will want to spend time with your father,' he explained.

'I fly to Sydney tomorrow and on to Auckland Friday,' Edward Sheldon interrupted, enjoying her discomfort. 'I won't get back to Tullamarine until an hour and a half before my flight out on Sunday. Provided you can get her there by 6.30 in the evening, she'll miss nothing.'

'It could be done . . .?' Drew agreed, turning to her, his expressive right eyebrow lifting a fraction.

Cynthia abruptly remembered that Shakespeare's Sonnet 94 was actually a condemnation of those who take advantage of our emotions to make fools of us while concealing their own, which made it even more appropriate. Drew Mitchell would let nothing stand in his way, not disappointment, nor his own feelings.

'You obviously fly?' she said inanely, her mind still unresponsive. She needed time to think. The dossier prepared by the private inquiry firm had not mentioned a pilot's licence.

'Yes. It is very useful for preliminary surveys of prospective areas.'

Out of the corner of her eye, she could see her father noting another useful talent, but she ignored him. Her mind had woken, realised how hard Drew was working to repair the damage and decided he deserved her aid.

'What time tomorrow?' she asked.

'I could file a flight plan for a two o'clock take off. We can have a light lunch in the pilot's lounge before that, so I'll pick you up at eleven-thirty?'

It was obvious that her gaffe had destroyed their unspoken tryst for tonight so she must be content with postponement. She nodded her acceptance. Drew acknowledged her agreement, turned away and accepted his coat from the maid before thanking her parents for the invitation and making his goodbyes. He seemed the only one entirely comfortable with the situation and his departure left a small pool of silence.

Cynthia stood, watching the door close behind him. There was something offbeat in Drew's reaction. He had already guessed her father's involvement in the invitation, so her revelation of it would have come only as a confirmation. Her presumption in dictating his future involvement in the aid agency would have amused him. She knew him well enough to be sure of that—which left only her remark about getting the truth about what happened in the mine.

She had been open about that from the beginning and, in spite of her occasional doubts, still believed that Drew had rescued her on the high plains. Had he laughed at her gaffe, or poked gentle fun at her, she would not have been surprised. The total lack of emotion on his face indicated that he was hiding a strong reaction, but she had no idea what it was. All she could do was to feel a little dazed at how inadequate her responses had been and how sad the ending.

Shakespeare came to her rescue once more and she smiled ruefully. Tonight was either 'Much ado about nothing' or else 'Love's labour's lost'. She was not sure which.

7

A felon at the bottom step of the gallows must feel this same mixture of reluctance and impatience, Cynthia decided, as she waited for Drew to arrive the following morning. The rational part of her mind prayed that the appointed time would pass without his appearance. That he would take offence at her gaffe and it would all end without further ado. It would make the immediate future difficult, but she would survive. The alternative simply terrified her.

Not enough to still completely the clamour from that corner of her mind that was unequivocally his. She would have to build high walls to contain that area. Anything less would be futile and any breach she would have to seal immediately, lest the memories of Drew Mitchell escape and batter down every rational defence.

At eleven thirty-five, she began to relax. Punctuality was so much a part of his character that even five minutes was proof that he was not coming. She turned to the overnight bag and make-up case on the settee. Unpacking and rehanging her clothes in the wardrobe would be the full stop of the affair. There was no longer any point in creasing her clothing unnecessarily . . .

The first of the two-tone notes from the door chime froze her in mid movement, as did the second. It made her turn back towards the door in discrete steps, like the movement caught by the flash of a strobe light in a discotheque. The effect on her pulse triggered an adrenaline rush that spread an arctic chill though her entire body.

It was six steps to the front door from where she stood. Each one took an effort of will to make . . . and opening the door drained her willpower to a point where she felt hollow.

'Hello,' he said coolly. 'I'm sorry that I'm late.'

He offered no reason, merely standing there with a look of polite inquiry on his face. She catalogued his appearance, more as an excuse to avoid thought than anything else.

The favoured blue Country shirt hid beneath a navy blue bomber jacket in polished cotton. The zippered front was open and she could see the broad plaited leather belt at the waist of his moleskin trousers. A dark polished brown, it matched his boat shoes.

'I didn't think that you were coming,' she said, so softly that he unconsciously leant towards her.

'But you packed your bags, just in case . . .'

She glanced over her shoulder automatically. It gave her the opportunity to break the contact of their eyes.

'Yes,' she agreed.

'Then we'd best get moving.'

They discussed the weather on the drive to the airport, each exchange making the next a little easier. She had no idea what he was thinking, but he had obviously decided that he would handle the situation on a casual acquaintanceship basis with no latitude given for anything beyond. She made two tentative approaches. He rebuffed both very gently, but quite firmly. His reserve now seemed impervious to anything she might offer.

The pilot's lounge was light and airy, with large plate glass windows for viewing the aircraft park and apron. True to his word, Drew had arranged a light lunch of salad and cold meats and they sat so she could watch the activity before them. He seemed to know many of the pilots and all of the staff, so their table was a popular pausing spot.

'You seem to have a lot of friends here,' she commented politely.

A quizzical lift of that right eyebrow was his only response, forcing her to re-examine the situation, an exercise aided by her reflection in the plate glass. She had chosen her outfit with care. A soft open-necked white blouse, with a crimson silk bandanna folded tightly and closely knotted at her throat, tailored beige slacks and polished tan flat-heeled shoes achieved exactly the casual elegance she had sought. She smiled to herself at the subtlety of the compliment she had just received. Perhaps

136

she would still have the last say . . . ?

Their aircraft was a high-wing monoplane. She did not recognise the type, but guessed that it was one of the ubiquitous Cessnas— something 185 according to the worn label on the instrument panel. The pilot and passenger sat side-by-side and the cabin was not pressurised. Drew stowed her two bags, saw her seated comfortably in the right-hand seat, checked her seat belt and carried out his pre-flight checks with a seemingly casual expertise that did not conceal the thoroughness of his preparation. He provided her with a light set of earphones to listen in to the radio traffic with the tower as the aircraft rolled from the apron onto the taxiway. Everything happened with a deceptive smoothness that was the real measure of his ability.

The take off appeared effortless. The tail lifted as the speed increased, levelling the aircraft and giving her a better view forward, then the ground fell away below her on either side as if by its own volition. The aircraft rolled into a faultless one gee turn towards the exit corridor and the earth tilted up outside her window, the false gravity creating the illusion that it moved rather than the aircraft. A few adjustments of the trimming wheels, the rate of climb and a long careful look around later, he engaged the auto pilot and relaxed in his seat beside her.

'That was very impressive,' she said.

137

'Thank you. I enjoy flying.'

'I would call that a statement of the obvious.'

He smiled at that. A relaxed smile. Score one for me, she congratulated herself smugly.

They had now come full circle, she realised, but this time she knew precisely the risks she was taking in coming with Drew Mitchell. He had cast the die by keeping his word this morning and she had now waded her Rubicon to enter a dangerous land where events would move beyond her control. His reserve was the first obstacle. Once that was breached, 'the game's afoot,' to quote Shakespeare's 'Henry V'.

She had a sudden vivid memory of her father's face in the firelight as he read Shakespeare to her as a child. He had brought the plays to life in his readings, making them, and the sonnets, her favourites ever since.

Drew unfolded the air navigation map and showed her their route across the mountain range. They would overfly Mansfield and veer north enough to cover the area of the Bogong High Plains where she had become lost.

'It will give you a clearer picture of the terrain before we ride up the mountains behind Mitchell's Run,' he explained.

She had never flown in a light plane before. It was more immediate than in an airliner. The ground was closer, its details clearer, and there was a sensation of speed in the rush of the outside air and the occasional buffet of turbulence. At Drew's urging, she took the controls for a while, gingerly changing height and direction under his coaching, but she relinquished them gratefully. It was harder than he made it look, and she was content to admire the scenery below as he identified the towns and the catchment area of Eildon Reservoir. It was more relaxing than car travel. The autopilot did the work of maintaining direction and height, leaving Drew only the task of constant vigilance, his eyes routinely scanning the instrument panel and the sky around them. She felt confident in his ability.

'When did you learn to fly?' she asked, curious why the inquiry agency failed to uncover the fact.

'A friend of the family was a night-fighter pilot during the Second World War. He operated a small aerial service and I used to fly with him as a boy. I had my hours in before I went to England to study and sat for my licence over there. I qualified on a couple more aircraft during the time I spent in South Africa and had my licence endorsed when I came home.'

She nodded her acknowledgment. 'He must have been a good teacher.'

'He was the highest scoring Australian of the night-fighter pilots . . . and he survived,' he said, smiling at the memory of the man.

Another relaxed smile. It is not so hard, she

thought. He had already revealed how much he cared. All she had to do was retrieve her blunder of last night. She could not do it frontally. He would never allow it. She would have to make last night seem unimportant.

The memory of a moment when he was loading her bags into the plane popped unbidden into her mind and she had to discipline herself into not laughing aloud. He had been bending forward and the bomber jacket had ridden up his back. She had been standing behind him with the other bag and had stifled an urge to lean forward and cup the tightened muscles of his right buttock in her hand. It would certainly have broken the ice, she thought, laughter bubbling away inside her. She kept her face turned away from him and concentrated on the scenery below until she could control her features once more.

'That's Mansfield coming up on your side,' he said. 'I don't want to sacrifice any altitude, but we'll swing round in a circle so that you can see it from above. Where we held the race is on the far side.'

He flicked off the autopilot and banked the aircraft away to the north, broadening the sweep of the circle to encompass the outlying area of Sheepyard Flat.

'That's where they hold the Great Mountain Race,' he said pointing down past her as the aircraft banked to the right to begin its sweep. 'They race over a fixed track, up the hill and down across the creek. It's great spectator stuff,' he admitted, his finger tracing the route. 'The local tourist association started it after the success of the film, "The Man from Snowy River". It's gone from strength to strength since. The Mountain Cattleman's Association has run the Cattleman's Cup since the fifties. It's at Omeo next year, closer to Mitchell's Run. The four branches of the Association run it in turn on a different property each year.'

They circled Mansfield twice, increasing altitude while Drew continued the travelogue commentary, before resuming the northeast track towards the mountains proper.

'It will get a little bumpy for a while,' he warned. 'If you tighten your seat belt, a little, you won't notice it as much.'

She followed his advice just in time, for the next few minutes made her grateful that she was not subject to motion sickness. Drew kept checking her appearance, particularly after one quite exciting plunge forced an unladylike squeal through her clenched teeth. Then they were past the turbulence on the windward side of the mountains and the aircraft settled back to steady flight.

She grinned her relief at him. 'I'm not sure I'd like to go through something that you considered more than "a little bumpy",' she said. 'That was exciting enough for me. Will there be more?'

'Only a couple of patches. None as bad.'

141

He re-engaged the auto pilot, she had not noticed him take control in the turbulence, and relaxed, a smile hinting that he had been worried about her ability to cope with the movement.

It was very pleasant now. The aircraft noise was no longer intrusive and his initial reserve had thawed to the point where they chatted comfortably about anything that came to mind. Sometimes it was about things he pointed out below, at other times about totally unrelated topics. He was genuinely interested in her opinions, often offering his own wry and offbeat insights in clarification. The dry sense of humour surfaced often and she strove to match it. She could sense them becoming friends, another gift of value from this man. One she had not anticipated. It did not occur to her to remember what Beth had said about friendship . . . at least not then.

'We are coming up to the area where you became lost,' Drew said, pointing ahead. 'I'll circle over the Stockman's Hut and we can follow your track from there.'

There was not a cloud in the sky now and the sun was shining brilliantly. The air was like crystal and she felt as if she could reach out and touch the tops of the trees below. Wildflowers, blooming amid the alpine gums, had tinted the uniform olive green with colour. He had been right in saying that an aerial view gave a better perception of terrain. It was remarkably easy to follow the marked trail from this altitude.

'That's where I think you went into the creek. The track bends around it and there is a deep pool in the corner below that steep bank.'

Her eyes followed where his pointing finger traced the run of the creek.

'Your friends would have been around the bend of the track, making it appear as if they were off to your left,' he continued. 'The pool would have cushioned your fall when the snow bank collapsed. There's a spring in the rock, just there, and the pool never freezes over completely.'

She could see the wetness of the spring and the pool it formed.

'You would have come out on the low side and followed the slope down to here.' He pointed to a swathe of cleared land. It was on the left side of the creek. 'You did quite well. That's a fair distance in sodden clothing. There's an overhang near the entrance to the mine just this side of the creek. You told the Alpine Patrol and the Police that you sheltered there.'

'You know a lot about what I did,' she accused.

'I read the reports before we dined together,' he said, smiling at her suspicions. 'I know the country rather well and it wasn't hard to put a location to your description. The

National Parks people checked it out rather thoroughly as well. You were not entirely discreet in the people you chose to tell the truth. We all noted your subsequent interest in Andrew Mitchell.'

His tone was matter of fact and nonjudgmental.

'Your survival in the conditions at the time was rather unusual. It generated a lot of interest in you by the people who knew, and the inquiry people didn't exactly make themselves invisible in a close-knit community.'

He was not condemning her, but it did not make her feel very clever to have her actions discussed and analysed so casually.

'I feel rather a fool,' she admitted.

'Don't,' he replied, his tone definite. 'The common reaction was to admire your loyalty to Andrew.'

'Was that your reaction?'

'I'd been out bush and had just caught up with the gossip when Jo rang. Beth had researched you thoroughly after the rescue and I recognised Jo as your business partner. I knew they had just aired the life style program about Mitchell's Run, so it was not a coincidence. I made a phone call to Dulcie and you know the rest.'

The plane had come round to the heading he wanted for the strip at Mitchell's Run so he levelled the wings and they flew away from the area of her adventure.

'You were expecting Jo at Mitchell's Run,' she persisted, giving him the chance to explain his surprise in the kitchen of Mitchell's Run. She had her own thoughts on the matter since she found out that he had arranged the booking.

'Yes. There was a colour photograph of you both in one of the social gossip columns in Beth's file. I was not really prepared to meet you.'

'I didn't expect the invitation to Mansfield,' she said, following the train of thought. 'You made it quite clear by the lake that you didn't want to see me again.'

'I got trapped by my own cleverness,' he said, grinning with embarrassment. 'After Jo rang, I added your name to the invitations before I left for Mitchell's Run. She had given the shop as her address, so I used that. When I got back, I found that Beth had posted all the invitations. I was still very embarrassed by my overreaction to you, so I decided to make amends by following it with the telephone call.'

He is lying to me again, Cynthia thought. So simple a reason as embarrassment would never have made him call her. There had to be something pressing enough to overcome his pride. He might be half in love with her now, but then, he hardly knew her.

That thought brought another in its train.

If Drew Mitchell was not the man who rescued her from the snow, then Andrew

Mitchell must have been a man far ahead of his time in his attitude to women . . . ?

She turned in her seat until she faced across the aircraft and looked directly at her companion, her mind grappling with the underlying logic of her conclusion. At first glance, it seemed unassailable. The anachronism of a Victorian era gentleman treating a woman as equal had not occurred to her before. He may have treated her as a lady, but never as an equal. There was an instant surge of elation that she had found the flaw in his charade. Then her father's words came back to her, 'he's too smart to be caught out that easily'.

'Did Andrew ever think about marriage?' she asked, mainly to test the theory.

'Yes,' Drew responded, a startled glance revealing his surprise at the change in subject. 'A local girl, who married money after Andrew disappeared. She spent a lot of time searching for him when he went missing. Became a leading suffragette later in life.'

Perhaps her logic was wasted. A budding suffragette would find a man who treated her as an intellectual equal very attractive. She filed the thought away for the moment. Her father was right. There would be no simple way to unravel the puzzle of Andrew Mitchell.

They passed the main ridge of the mountains and the high plains fell behind as the aircraft descended steeply into a valley that

146

led eastward and then broadened to sweep south. A spur of the lesser mountains to the east left a narrow gap as the only communication with the much broader and deeper river valley beyond. In the distance, about twenty kilometres to the east, she could see the waters of the Dartmouth Reservoir.

'Mitchell's Run,' Drew said, pointing ahead at the cluster of buildings clinging to the southern slope of the valley the aircraft was descending.

From above it was easier to see how the buildings straddled the upper of two lesser ridges running parallel to the escarpment of the high plains and how the large dam created the ornamental lake. Something she had not noticed during her earlier stay was a small cemetery, a hundred metres further up the ridge from the homestead and separated from it by another building.

Drew noticed her interest and mistook its focus. 'Andrew built that before he went to England,' he said, pointing to the building below the cemetery. 'I live there now.'

The plane banked quite steeply and spiralled down towards the bush strip below the lake. She could see a battered 4WD waiting for them and a figure beside it waving. Drew waggled the wings in acknowledgment, then concentrated on the task of landing down slope into the light breeze. It was a little like going down in an elevator as he held the nose of the aircraft up and allowed it to mush downward, killing the forward speed to the point where the stall light blinked furiously. At a moment that seemed almost too late, he dropped the nose and made a perfect three-point landing. The aircraft rolled to a stop right next to the 4WD. It was a demonstration of flying skill Cynthia could not fault. However, she would have preferred to watch it from the ground.

I'll bet you could do with a cuppa after that,' Dulcie said as she opened Cynthia's door from the outside.

'Jack is in the middle of a foaling,' she explained. 'He'll come down and pick up Drew later. It will take him half an hour to put his toy to bed, so we'll go on home to settle you in. Drew! Put the bags in the back,' she ended peremptorily as the latter came around the nose of the plane to join them.

Drew grinned and obeyed, tugging an imaginary forelock. Cynthia got out of her seat to step down onto the hard packed earth of the apron and found herself enveloped in a firm hug. Dulcie had a country smell, a pleasant mixture of domestic and rural odours, none of them strong.

'Goldilocks suits you,' Dulcie said, as they parted.

'But it's not my name,' Cynthia responded.

'No. It's not,' the other woman agreed, giving Cynthia a thoughtful look. 'Good on you. Don't let him dictate to you. He does it too naturally.'

The Mitchell women were an independent lot, Cynthia decided. They probably had to be, was her second thought on the subject.

The first person they saw when they reached the homestead was Peter, the agricultural college student who had come second in the race, one of her dancing partners at Mansfield. He greeted her warmly, a red flush of embarrassment not detracting from his grin. Stripped to the waist and smeared with blood, he seemed oblivious of everything but his news.

'It's a filly,' he announced proudly. 'Another of Shaka's get. She's as black as the ace of spades and as lovely as sin. Do you want to see her? I've cleaned up the mess.'

'She can wait till we've had a cuppa,' Dulcie decided for them. 'Cynthia's just endured one of Drew's fancy landings and not all of the mess is cleaned up,' she ended, looking meaningfully at Peter's state. 'Clean yourself up and you can join us in the kitchen. Tell Jack that Drew is still down at the plane, though I imagine he'll probably walk up before either of you get there.'

There was little doubt in Cynthia's mind who controlled what happened around the homestead itself.

8

'It is almost a shrine,' Cynthia said, her voice unconsciously hushed in respect. She had just entered the separate building that had been Andrew's home at Mitchell's Run and was now Drew's.

The wood panelled room in front of her was part library, part study, and part sitting room. A Zulu shield of pure white ox hide and assegai hung on the wall opposite. A Martini-Henry rifle, with fixed bayonet, flanked it on the right. A second lever-action rifle, with a brass breechblock and tubular magazine, hung below that. On the left hung a regimental colour and a white tropical helmet not unlike a London Bobby's helmet. The cap badge of the helmet struck a familiar chord, but she could not place it for the moment. More interestingly, in one of the glass bookshelves below the decorations was a row of the leather bound journals. Each one exactly like that in which she had seen Andrew Mitchell writing when she woke for the second time.

'They look familiar,' she said, crossing the room to the cabinet.

'You might find the ninth one interesting,' Drew said, closing the door and joining her.

They all had numbers on the spine, hand done in gold leaf. She opened the cabinet and withdrew the journal marked by the Roman numeral 'IX'. It fell open at the red silk-ribbon bookmark sewn into the spine. A neat, cursive script, the letters even and precise, filled one page. On the other page was a detailed Indian ink sketch of Mitchell's Run during the construction of the dam wall. The trees were less imposing and some of the newer buildings were missing, but it was so exquisitely detailed that she could recognise the windows of the room in which they stood. Below the main drawing were a cross-section of the dam wall and some spidery calculations of earthwork volume.

She could read the writing on the opposite page easily. It described the construction of the stonework spill tower in the middle of the dam. The tower fed a stone-lined runway tunnel into the creek below the wall. It referred to the small neat calculations in the margin for runoff strength and velocity. A row of question marks followed the calculation of energy loss.

She leafed through the pages, noting the quality and number of the sketches. They ranged in size and content from full-page landscapes to thumbnail drawings of wildflower stamens. The quality of the detail was the only uniform aspect. It was so fascinating that she was barely aware of Drew's presence. An oddity that did not strike her at the time, for she could almost hear

Andrew Mitchell's voice as she read the words that he had written a hundred years ago.

After a dozen pages, she paused and looked around, returning to the present almost with a start. For all of its shrine-like characteristics, the room had a lived-in feel. There was no dust and the small table next to the huge leather club chair carried three modern books, a magazine and the Cambridge text of Shakespeare's complete works. The same one she had used at high school.

'Yes,' Drew responded to her questioning look. 'I've been refreshing my memory of the sonnets. My bedroom is through there and I've added a studio and office as well.'

'Studio?'

'If you continue through that door, you'll see for yourself.'

She took his advice and found herself on a raised balcony in a large well-lit room two stories high. They had excavated the floor into the reverse slope of the ridge and the mansard line of the roof and rear wall was made entirely of glass. There was a clever arrangement of tracked blinds to close it off and an ornate cast iron pot-bellied stove for winter warmth. To her left, on the same level was a mezzanine landing with a massive four-poster bed. Beyond it, she could see the entrance to a walk-in wardrobe and en-suite.

On her right, the landing continued and became a neat modern office, complete with computer and modem. Immediately below her, on the main floor, was a large artist's easel carrying a covered canvas. It was all rather unexpected and a complete contrast from the room she had just left.

'May I?' she asked, indicating the stair down to the studio floor.

'Of course,' he said.

She descended the spiral staircase, which ended under the mezzanine floor facing a wall hung with unframed photographs and topographical maps. In front of them was a large drafting table, complete with pantograph drafting machine. Lying on the table was a canvas stretched on a frame. Moving closer to it, she could see that it was covered with the fine perspective lines and heavier charcoal outlines of a landscape. A sheet covered with calculations with the answers in degrees of angle lay beside it. She studied it for a while and realised that these were the perspective angles of the various features of the landscape on the canvas.

'I can see why people might suggest that your painting is more like drafting,' she said, looking over her shoulder with a smile.

He returned the smile a little uncertainly. It was the second time she had seen him other than supremely self confident and it was slightly shocking. Yet there was an appeal to it that touched her heart.

'Is that a painting that you are working on?'

she asked, pointing at the covered canvas on the easel.

'Yes,' he said and removed the light cotton cover.

It was another landscape, the unfinished part showing the perspective lines and underlying charcoal drawing. The finished part stopped her in her tracks. It was a superb mass of detail that made it effective at any distance. This was no photographic representation of a bush scene. It was instead a loving capture of the essence of the Australian bush. A marriage of engineer and artist—the engineer had created the skeleton and the artist had then clothed it in glory.

'Whoever criticised this was a fool,' she breathed, her eyes gleaming with unshed tears from the ache of seeing something so purely beautiful.

'I guess I am at times,' he said quietly.

All of her feelings for this man, which had become so oddly muted during the day, flowered into vibrant being and she spun on her heel to face him. She was blindly intent on embracing him, on comforting him, on seeking her own comfort in his arms.

He was not there. He had moved unnoticed beyond the drafting table and was kneeling down to retrieve something. The momentum of her intent died and the moment passed, leaving in its stead the half recognition that something had changed. That some new factor had entered the equation between them. A very elusive thing, whatever it was, slipping slyly beyond her perception the moment she tried to examine it directly.

'This might interest you,' he said, straightening and placing a mid-sized canvas on the table between them.

It was a battle scene, showing scarlet-jacketed men wearing the tropical white helmets identical to the one in the other room. There was a kneeling front rank with bayonets fixed and, behind them, a second rank firing over a parapet of stacked bags. All bar one were firing Martini-Henry rifles in a volley into the massed Zulus. In spite of the skeins of powder smoke obscuring parts of the scene, the detail was so fine that she could see the individual expressions. Andrew Mitchell was there, firing the other rifle on the wall as part of the volley. Her first thought was that Drew had painted the scene, but then she recognised the age of the paint and compared it mentally to the Indian-ink drawings in the journals.

'Andrew painted this . . .?' she said wonderingly.

'Yes. That is Rorke's Drift. You can recognise John Chard and Gonville Bromhead. He describes it in detail in the sixth journal. That and Isandlwhana.'

She held the painting in her hand so that she could compare it with the one in the easel. The differences were minor and completely swamped by the similarities. Only the age of the paint identified one against the other.

'Heredity runs powerfully in your family,' she said thoughtfully. 'It carries talent as well as appearance.'

'I was lucky. I had a worthwhile model.'

'I doubt that anyone who knows you thinks of you as anything less than a rather unique individual. Heredity may have provided the raw material, but you are your own man.'

She had not really considered the matter until that instant, but she knew with utter certainty that she had just said the right thing, for not only was it true, it was what Drew needed to hear.

Her reward was a long level look. One in which she felt herself carefully weighed in the balance. He gave no clue as to the result. He just replaced the cover on his own painting and returned Andrew's painting to its storage and suggested that it was now time for them to see the new filly in the stable.

The quietness between them was a measure of the change and she simply waited for him to lead the way. The forefront of her mind grappled with this new puzzle whilst that area which had become his exulted. This internal partition of loyalties had now become so familiar that she accepted it as normal and could barely remember the time when it did not exist. Anything that had been before seemed to have been in a different life, had happened to a different person. This was the first time she acknowledged the changes that had been wrought and recognised them as irrevocable.

The young filly stood on shaky legs at her mother's side, the latter a chestnut mare with a white blaze. Peter had called it correctly. The foal was a total unrelieved black, her coat already gleaming from the attention she had received from mother and the attending humans.

'We'll have to name her,' Jack said, a massive, yet gentle, man with fair sandy hair and odd green eyes.

'Cyn.' Drew's voice carried a quiet authority.

'As in Original Sin?' Dulcie asked, with a knowing glance at Cynthia.

'No. As in C, Y, N. In honour of our guest.'

Smiles confirmed Drew's pronouncement and to Cynthia went the honour of conferring the name by hugging the foal's neck. The mare looked curiously at the strange antics of the humans who attended her and accepted them as just another oddity of the race. She nudged Cynthia gently away with her soft velvety nose and sniffed her offspring carefully to assure herself that no harm had been done.

'We'll leave you alone now, girl,' Dulcie agreed. 'It's time for us to eat as well.'

They trooped up to the main house, Dulcie taking Cynthia's arm and leading the way, the men following dutifully behind.

There were no paying guests so they ate casually at the kitchen table, the warmth of the stove combating the growing chill of the mountain evening. The conversation was relaxed, ranging mainly over such rural topics that would interest Cynthia. Peter chimed in with a description of a lecturer at the agricultural college, which would surely have been grounds for slander if the man concerned had heard.

Drew was very quiet. He cast no pall on the conversation, smiling occasionally at their remarks and giving brief answers in response to direct questions. He looked very relaxed to Cynthia, content to just listen and watch. The others obviously found his behaviour normal. She had to remind herself how little she really knew about him.

'Which horses are you going to take tomorrow?' Jack asked, speaking directly to Drew.

'Are they all back from Mansfield?'

'Yes. The Thompson boys dropped them off this morning.'

'We'll take the two we used there. Cynthia is used to the mare and the gelding is a willing enough worker. Old Ginger hasn't been out for a while. He can carry the gear. If we get lost, he'll bring us home.'

'What time?'

'Straight after breakfast. Seven o'clock?' he

looked across at her and made it a direct question.

She nodded, reminding herself that this was country hours and breakfast would be out of the way before the sun made work possible outside.

'I'll help Cynthia pack her saddle bags,' Dulcie offered. 'You'll be taking two swags.'

'Yes. I will take my own. Put out another three-quarter one and add an extra blanket. It is still chilly up there.'

Cynthia suddenly realised that they had been discussing the sleeping arrangements, that swags were a canvas-covered bedroll with a built-in mattress. She glanced quickly at Drew, but he was not looking at her. Last night had left her with her own ideas as to what the sleeping arrangements would be on their overnight camp . . . and they did not include the need for an extra blanket.

The intensity of her feelings for Drew had returned to full strength from the moment in the studio and the contrast made their lethargy earlier in the afternoon even more difficult to explain. Unbidden from her memory sprang something Beth had said; 'I had a terrible crush on him when we were younger. It drove me to distraction until he made us friends instead'. She had not understood it at the time, merely marking it mentally for later consideration. Events had then driven it from her mind. It suggested a deliberate act on

Drew's part . . .

'When will you be back?' Dulcie asked.

'A late lunch Sunday would be handy. Say, one o'clock? We need to reach Melbourne about five so Cynthia can see her father before he flies out.'

This led to a discussion about her father's work in Africa, with Dulcie the one to understand immediately the impact that it had made on his family. Jack and Peter defended him stoutly, citing the need for such aid and its humanitarian aspect. Drew was largely silent and she caught him looking at her in that considering way of his that was so disconcerting. His occasional comments more a search for confirmation than judgmental, and they showed clearly the depth of his existing knowledge.

'He's actually trapped,' he said, countering one of Dulcie's accusations of selfishness. 'He no longer has a choice. He has become an essential man. It probably crept up on him before he realised it. His only escape now is to find someone who can take his place. The very things that make him good at what he is doing are now the things that make it impossible for him to escape.'

'I don't understand,' Cynthia said.

'His skills as a manager, his knowledge of the system, his ability to get things done have all dug a pit from which he can't escape,' Drew explained. 'He makes the difference between

160

people living and dying right now. Not just at some time in the future—though he affects that as well—but right now! In the time that he has been away, women and children have probably died, purely because he was not there to make the difference. It is very hard to balance the needs of a family against that. I feel very sorry for him.'

'He sees you as a possible replacement . . .' Cynthia said slowly, recognising the reason for her father's desperation at last.

'Yes. I know, but it is not a replacement that he needs,' Drew said, and there was something in his tone that eluded her.

'Well, I know something too,' Jack said, coming to his feet. 'It's time for bed. Those damned cows will still be at the gate at five a.m. Excuse me, won't you. I'm off to bed now.'

The group broke up quickly at that, Dulcie going with Cynthia to the guests' suite, the same room she had occupied before. It had once been the major bedroom of the house. She picked up a swag from the storeroom and then stayed long enough to show Cynthia how to roll her outer clothes into the swag and pack her personal effects into the two saddlebags. She insisted on lending Cynthia a long rider's coat and a nearly new Akubra hat.

'If the weather changes, you'll be thankful for both, and it happens very quickly up there.'

Cynthia showered in the en-suite bathroom, donned the simply cut, white satin nightgown she had packed specially and sat brushing her hair in front of the dressing table. The nightly routine was always a time for reflection as the mindless brush strokes calmed her thoughts and relaxed the tensions of the day.

Jo was right. Just being around Drew Mitchell was exhausting. In a little over a week, he had turned her life upside down and taken her from confident ignorance to thoughtful uncertainty. She no longer knew what it was she wanted, nor what she was prepared to pay to get it, but she had the sense that an accounting would come soon. She suspected that Drew Mitchell was far ahead of her, that he knew exactly what it was that he wanted and precisely the price that he would pay.

Her problem was that she was not even sure what it was that she felt about Drew. He excited, challenged, and frustrated her. She could admire him while distrusting his motives and lusting after his body, all at the same time. It was like nothing else that she had ever known, yet it was hauntingly familiar, as if she had been searching for it all of her life. It was tempting to believe that she had fallen in love with Drew Mitchell. However, if that was so, then the only thing that this had in common with romantic love, as she understood it, was she could no longer imagine life without him.

Yet marriage was still impossible.

Her father would not quibble at the cost of

restoring Mitchell's Run. It would be a good investment, with Dulcie, Jack and Peter providing expert management. More importantly, it would free Drew for the aid agency and her father could step aside with honour intact. Drew would sacrifice himself gladly for Mitchell's Run and she would take over her mother's role as an aid agency widow.

She would never accept that!

It would seem that Drew himself was not without doubts. Nothing else could explain his attempt to defuse their relationship by replacing the sexual tension with friendship. She had not understood Beth's comment about Drew making them friends until he had shown just how effective a ploy that it could be. He had miscalculated by showing her his painting, otherwise she would never have guessed. He had only partly succeeded in recovering the ground since. His defence of her father had been his reaction to that failure. He was warning her off, telling her as clearly as he could that it was unprofitable for her to continue. It was, in itself, a confirmation of how much he cared.

There was another possibility. The man she had met in the mine had proven himself capable of extreme subtlety and Drew had used her own perceptiveness to tease her. If the two were the same man, then he would be adept enough to set her up to believe that she had divined all this by herself, using her own cleverness against her. It was a sobering thought.

His final comment, that her father did not want a replacement, puzzled her. It was something that he expected her to understand, but she did not—yet!

Her hair finished, she switched out the light, opened the blinds and slipped into bed. Outside bright moonlight illuminated the waters of the dam and dappled the leaves of the gums on the far side. Beyond she could see the dark loom of the far slope of the valley. She was not ready for sleep, though she understood that the morning would come all too soon.

Reading Andrew Mitchell's journals had made him real for the first time since that night in the mine. He had faded slowly into a shadowy figure from the past, with no reality beyond the words of others. His own words had changed that. He was now, once more, a flesh and blood man. The pattern of his thoughts had reached out and touched her mind, so that she could understand the hold he had on the Mitchell family. His journals were the gospel they lived by.

She would not have noticed the figure standing at the edge of the shadowed porch if he had not moved. He stepped forward just enough that the moonlight illuminated his features and stood looking out over the waters of the dam. It was Drew. He had donned a long dark coat against the chill of the night. It made him blend into the darkness so that only his face was distinct. He was possibly thinking similar thoughts to hers, weighing the cost of losing all of this to re-establish Mitchell's Run. If he went to Africa, he would become the essential man in her father's place, trapped by the same imperatives. It was not a choice she envied.

He turned and looked directly at her window, his features once more shadowed. She had the immediate sense that he could actually see her in spite of the shadows. She half moved to respond but he turned quite abruptly and walked away, the sound of his footsteps somehow lost in the silence.

The sound of the kitchen door opening and closing came a moment later and there was a sudden bloom in the darkness of the passage as the light came on. In the silence, she had even heard the click of the light switch. She lay there for a moment undecided, then threw back the covers. The matching coat for her nightgown was on the end of the bed and she padded barefoot along the passageway to the kitchen.

Drew had his back to her, pouring boiling water from the cast iron kettle into a teapot. The long coat was missing. He had probably left it outside, hanging on the verandah.

'I'd like a cup too,' she said.

He went still for a second, his only reaction

165

to the surprise of hearing her voice.

'There are mugs in the cabinet to your left. Get one for me as well, if you would.'

She handed them to him and he half filled each with boiling water and put them on the stove surround to pre-warm.

'Can't sleep?' he asked, as he collected milk from the fridge and sugar from the bench.

No,' she said. 'I saw you on the porch and heard you come in, so I thought I would join you.'

'On the porch?' he said.

'Yes,' she answered. 'You were looking out over the dam and then you turned away and came in.'

'Oh,' he said noncommittally, and changed the subject. 'I've been re-reading Andrew's last journal. He mentions a find much closer to Mitchell's Run. Unfortunately, he gives very little in the way of detail, just that he could see the homestead and that he found it on the way back from the high plains. It's on the last page. He probably took the next volume of the journal with him when he disappeared.'

'May I see?'

'Of course. I'll go and get it. You pour the tea.'

'How do you like it?'

'White and two,' he said over his shoulder as he left.

The slow combustion stove kept the kitchen warm, making the brief waft of air from the door feel icy. The sudden chill made her nipples bud proudly. She glanced down, saw them tenting the fine fabric, and wondered idly if Drew would notice. The thought triggered a reaction that had little to do with the temperature and she could feel the colour rise to add a bloom to her cheeks.

Drew noted it immediately as he entered the room and turned back to ensure that the door was properly closed. It bought him the time to think before he turned to face her again. There was now an odd expression in his eyes. One she had no way of interpreting, but it had more than a touch of reluctance.

He pulled out a chair and put the book on the table, gesturing her to sit so he could lean over her shoulder and point out the passage. She was exquisitely conscious of his nearness and could feel the fan of his breath on her hair as he opened the book at the last page and she followed the trace of his finger to the final paragraph.

'Look,' she said. 'It ends in mid sentence, as if it would continue the next page. Did he often do that at the end of the journals?' She automatically assumed that Drew had read them all.

'Only once,' he confirmed. 'The description of the aftermath of Rorke's Drift carries on from Journal Six to Journal Seven.'

'Then he must have taken the other journal with him,' she said, turning to face him.

'It seems likely,' he agreed, their faces only inches apart and the expression in his eyes a message in itself.

It was a moment to last a lifetime. She knew that he was going to kiss her and then a new part of her life would begin. Oddly, she noted for the first time that there were amber and green flecks in the dark brown of his eyes. The creases in his lower lip were unevenly spaced and he had missed two tiny dark hairs at the right corner of his mouth when he had shaved this morning. Then his lips came closer and her eyes closed as she moved to meet them with her own.

The gentle touch of his lips on hers was like a dream kiss; something that happened on the very edge of perception, but it flowed through her body like an icy wave, destroying her awareness of anything else. Only their gentle insistence was real, coaxing her lips to part, the tip of his tongue sampling the nectar within. It was as it had been before. He demanded nothing. Everything was for her to cede willingly . . . and cede it she did, willingly and completely.

There was no haste, no jarring fumbles. They came together as long time lovers, each so familiar with the other that there was no necessity for words, just a total understanding of their needs. He made everything happen smoothly. Each sensation flowed into the other and become an integral part of the whole. She rose to her feet, still within his embrace, and he swept her up into his arms to carry her along the passage to her borrowed bed. He stood her beside it and eased the straps from her shoulders. Her nightclothes cascaded to the floor to pool her feet in white satin and she was naked before him. It presaged only by moments her first glimpse of his lean, hard, wholly magnificent body completely bared and the wonder of it almost stilled her breath. He bore her gently back onto the bed and they came together, a fusion of souls as much as of physical bodies. He filled deliciously what had become an aching void and this simple union of their flesh soared into a consummation of the love she never quite believed would be hers. It was an experience like nothing else; a mutual striving so perfectly synchronised as to defy description. Her climax seemed to still the earth in its rotation and her world shifted irrevocably into a new alignment.

Even better, if such a thing were possible, was the sensitivity that made him ease her descent into sated quiescence by cherishing her with his lips and his hands.

'Wow,' she said softly, her breath stirring the fine hair on the arm that held her in his embrace.

'That's a remarkably exact description,' he murmured and the gentle humour in his voice made it the perfect response.

169

'You are going to have to do that again,' she warned.

'Now?'

'M-m-m,' she considered. 'Soon.'

'Can I rest on my laurels for just a little while?'

'Only if you must,' she agreed, gurgling with suppressed laughter. 'Though I imagine that they'd be rather prickly.'

'Just what I need right now. A woman with a literal mind.'

She thrust her face into the hollow of his shoulder to stifle her laughter. She did not know how close Dulcie and Jack's bedroom was, nor where Peter slept. It would not be polite to find out by waking them.

The whispered nonsense that followed was as much a part of their lovemaking as had been the physical union that had preceded it. She could still feel the echoes of what they had done rattling around inside her. There had to be an outlet. She would have happily danced across the ceiling, if that were possible, so their whispered words were the socially acceptable alternative. Drew seemed to understand exactly her need, his dry humour the perfect foil to her physical exuberance.

It was only much later that she made him live up to his commitment. He indulged her in a slow, deliberate, second consummation that built inexorably to another climax that shook her body in huge, shuddering sighs. These

170

subsided slowly and the languor that followed led her naturally into sleep, her back folded into his body so that they lay like two spoons. His breath gently fanning the nape of her neck her was last conscious sensation.

For the moment, it no longer mattered why this had happened, or what Drew's motives were. It had happened and life would never be quite the same again. Tomorrow, she would be prey once more to doubts and would fear again what the future might bring. Tonight, right now, she was content, and that was enough.

9

Cynthia woke effortlessly to the distant bustle in the kitchen. She stretched luxuriously, flexing her body like a sated feline, taking up all the bed. Muscles she did not remember having protested sweetly. It felt great to be alive. In just a moment, she would join Drew in the kitchen, but first she would drown herself a little in the memory of last night. Her hands mimicked his of their own accord, caressing the sensitive areas of her body, forcing her to stifle what was almost a moan. She bit her lip, using the pain as a barrier to the temptation to abandon herself completely. It would be so easy. She must get up . . . now!

Her need for him became a spur and she dressed, taking enough time to ensure that her appearance would remind him that she had really been worthy of his best effort.

She need not have bothered. It was Dulcie in the kitchen and she found herself smoothly coopted into the task of preparing breakfast, though she suspected Dulcie could have done it more easily on her own.

'The men are out saddling the horses,' the older woman explained. 'I heard Drew come in at dawn. He was noisier than usual.' The twinkle in Dulcie's eyes warned Cynthia that Drew had wasted the effort. All she could do was smile a wry acknowledgment of the truth.

Her mind still cherished the wonder of last night, her lips curving into a smile at the memory of each particular moment as it passed in review, vivid recollections that were far too immediate to permit analysis. All she could do was enjoy them. It would take the passage of time for her to distance herself enough to be able to view them in the context of what they meant for her future. As if cued by the thought, Drew entered the kitchen and she discovered that a part of her was already single minded about the future.

'Good morning,' he said formally, a marginal lift of that damned right eyebrow making its own comment on the delicate flush that climbed to colour her cheeks.

'Good morning,' she responded, striving to

172

make her voice sound as normal as the sweet tension in her vocal chords would allow.

'You can turn around and go straight out again,' Dulcie instructed mock-sternly. 'Tell the other two that breakfast will be ready in fifteen minutes if they keep you out of the kitchen. You are distracting my helper.'

'. . . And if I stay?' Drew challenged.

'Then you won't ride up into the hills till mid morning,' Dulcie warned.

'I'd best be on my way then,' he agreed.

He lingered just long enough to capture Cynthia's right hand and raise it so that his lips brushed the inside of her wrist. Then he obeyed Dulcie.

'No one ever wins against him,' Dulcie said, only half censoriously. 'Even when he apparently concedes a point, he always adds that final touch that gives him the victory.'

Cynthia could not help but agree—her own experience mirrored Dulcie's words. Any future that included Drew Mitchell . . . she stopped!

She had no future that included Drew Mitchell. Last night, wonderful as it had been, changed nothing. She could not accept last night, or any number of nights exactly the same, as payment for the years of loneliness with Drew away in Africa.

It was not Drew's fault. He had tried hard to divert her attention. It was tempting to believe that he understood her fear of the loneliness.

He had viewed her mother with compassion and shown himself incredibly perceptive in reading the situation with her father at the dinner. It did not seem beyond him to see into her mind . . . she suddenly remembered her sense of his reluctance at the kitchen door last night and was convinced.

It was now her turn to bear the load of the impossible situation her search for the truth about Andrew Mitchell had created. It would have been far better to acknowledge him as dead than to confront his descendant, but it was too late for that now and she must deal with the result.

By the time the three men entered the kitchen for breakfast, the role that she would have to play was clear in her mind. Nothing must alert the others. She would play the love-struck fool until she could escape.

It was surprisingly easy. She just let that part of her mind that was his have its way; while she mentally stood back and observed everything with heightened sensitivity.

Young Peter was totally infatuated with her, but so over-awed by Drew that he had no thought of competing with the older man. Jack, probably alerted by Dulcie, was approvingly aware of the situation, smiling quietly to himself as he watched Drew operate. Dulcie remained the real danger. Impervious to Drew's charm, her native shrewdness honed by her experience as a B&B operator, she missed nothing!

Even Drew was not her equal—at least not this morning. There was a touch of smugness in his manner and, to Cynthia's sharply critical eyes, it was blunting his perception. Once out of Dulcie's sight, she might just be able to fool him.

There was little in the way of breakfast conversation, the three men efficiently destroying the neat stacks of toast as they cleaned the platters of eggs, bacon and sausages. Sharply aware of her own hunger, she kept apace for a while, then conceded defeat and sat with a steaming mug of tea whilst they plundered the surviving morsels. It was only when they had emptied every platter, and scoured each plate clean with toast that the three men sat back in their chairs and joined her in savouring the tea.

'I think I needed that,' Jack said unnecessarily. 'He's a damn hard boss. We've saddled the horses, checked the filly and her foal, old Ginger is loaded and the Alpine Parks people have been e-mailed about his route and camping plan. I'm glad he only gets up here occasionally, I'm not too sure that I'm young enough to keep up with him any more.'

The explosion of mirth from Peter and Drew, plus the mock commiseration from Dulcie, told Cynthia all she needed to know about the seriousness of Jack's complaint.

'It's all right, Jack,' she said. 'I understand.'

175

'Only because she's never had to work for you, you poor old sod!' Peter riposted with a laugh.

Cynthia hid herself in the good-humoured banter that followed. It was only a temporary respite. Soon, she and Drew would be alone together on the trail. Until then, she would have to maintain the facade of a thoroughly be-smitten woman.

'It's time for us to be on our way,' Drew said, glancing at the kitchen clock and coming to his feet. 'It's a fairly solid ride to get there with enough time to explore the mine today.'

She nodded and stood up. 'I'll get my things,' she agreed.

Their departure from the homestead went quite smoothly. Drew helped her mount, fussed about the length of her stirrups and the security of the saddle bags, before mounting himself and leading the way across the minor valley that separated the homestead from the mountains behind it.

It was exhilarating. The air was crisp, the post-dawn light soft and the horses frisky with the sense of a holiday from their normal routine. The mare pranced proudly before settling down to the comfortable lope that had impressed Cynthia so much outside Mansfield. The gelding was more phlegmatic, or more firmly under the control of his rider, and the packhorse, Ginger, was old enough to view the whole adventure quite placidly, though he too seemed to be enjoying the morning ride.

They rode along the valley of cleared land for two kilometres and paused at a gate in the fence that separated it from the tree line.

'This is our latest acquisition,' Drew said, indicating the mountain slope above them as he leaned from the saddle to open the gate. 'It was the original limit of Mitchell's Run; the lease ran right up onto the high plains, and as far to the east as the eye can see. Now all we have is this strip that reaches barely beyond the air strip.'

The edge of bitterness in his voice was barely discernible, but it was there and she wondered at the sense of ownership that could leap across generations. Only a rural family could understand it fully, she supposed. She looked back at the homestead and then up the slope that formed the escarpment of a plateau.

At its crown, for a third of the length, almost a kilometre, a cliff face of fissured rock jutted out like the battlements of a fortress. One particularly impressive parapet frowned immediately over the gate. The slope below the cliffs was too steep for grazing, with oddly stunted vegetation, compared to the tall alpine gums that grew thickly beyond the extent of the cliffs. You would buy this sort of land as an afterthought, as a buffer area rather than a core purchase. It was uncharacteristic of the careful planning that had marked the re-establishment of Mitchell's Run to this point.

'It fits what Andrew wrote about his last gold find,' she said musingly.

'Yes, unfortunately,' he agreed.

'Why is it unfortunate?'

'Do you want the full lecture, or will you be satisfied that there is an occasional slippage of strata at this point of the mountain range and this creates earth tremors and land slips. You can see by the lack of old vegetation that the slope is actually the rocky scree of previous falls, thinly covered by earth washed down from the plateau. To tunnel in this area would be extremely risky. The only way to get the gold would be by an open cut. It would be prohibitively expensive and could you imagine the reaction of the greenies to the scar it would create. I've prospected the surface area and found nothing. If Andrew found the gold there, then it is deep—and that's where it will have to stay.'

It was a long speech for him, yet it left her unconvinced. He had a reason for buying the land and mere technical difficulties would never deter him. It was too far away from the area of her rescue to be significant in that sense, but she would have to keep it in mind. Perhaps he could be driving a shaft from the other mine towards the unstable area. The distance might be shorter. She had no idea how extensive the diggings had been in the 1920s.

Beyond the gate, a faint trail curved away to

their right, cutting diagonally across the slope. Drew took the lead, allowing the gelding to make his own pace. Old Ginger followed placidly, the lead rope hardly necessary, and the mare seemed content to bring up the rear. Only the muffled fall of the hooves and the creak of leather disturbed the bush peace, apart from the distant cawing of a crow, hidden somewhere in the valley below them.

They climbed slowly, the trail zigzagging below the cliff in a series of switchbacks. The vegetation was low enough in places that she could see the valley below. Elsewhere it closed in and she could not see over it, even by standing in her stirrups. At each end of the zigzag, the thick stands of mountain gum formed a barrier, forcing the trail to turn back on itself. These were the only points where she was close enough to talk to Drew without raising her voice, so their conversation consisted of brief exchanges and long silences. It suited her. She could escape his direct scrutiny and relax during the transits of the slope.

Near the head of the slope, the trail followed the foot of the cliff until it reached a long fissure running up behind the parapet that guarded the gate. Here the trail turned into the cliff and became quite steep.

'Lean forward as much as you can,' Drew instructed and set the gelding scrambling up the trail. He had lengthened the lead rope and old Ginger waited until the rope was about to become taut before starting up the slope after the gelding. The mare followed without any urging from Cynthia as soon as the path was clear. It was quite exhilarating, especially when she emerged from the fissure and the view of the valley burst upon her. Drew was waiting, the two horses standing near the edge of the parapet. He motioned her alongside. The view was magnificent and she was surprised to see how far they had climbed. She could see beyond the valley that contained Mitchell's Run and into the broader river valley that she had seen from the plane. In the far distance, she could see the waters of the Dartmouth Reservoir.

'In Andrew's time, this parapet was higher. He mentions it because he sheltered under its overhang during a storm. My guess is that an earth tremor caused it to shear along the plane of the fissure and drop to close the overhang. You can see that this area is almost three metres below the rest of the ridge.'

What he said was obvious. The section on which they stood was level, but the rest of the cliff top, on the other side of the fissure, was higher than her head, even when she stood in the stirrup. The path that connected the head of the fissure and the main cliff top was man-made, cut into the rock in a series of steps broad enough for horses and cattle.

'I have found no one who remembers an

overhang, so it must have broken off not long after Andrew wrote about it,' Drew continued. 'One day, this whole area will probably tumble all the way down into the valley.'

'I don't think that I would like to be around when that happens.'

'Neither would I. It would probably break up once it got going and then the individual pieces would spread out. It would destroy anything in that arc.' He swung his arm to indicate what he meant.

Her eyes followed the sweep of his arm and saw that the trail they had ridden lay directly in the path of the potential rockslide. It was not a comforting thought.

She turned back from the view and found Drew looking directly at her. His gaze was level and considering, and she realised that his talk about the rockslide had been merely to assess her mood. Steeling herself, she returned his gaze, expecting him to say something. Instead he just turned the gelding away and led off up the path. The other two horses fell into line and the ride continued.

She had known that fooling him was going to be difficult, but she had not expected him to be aware of the change in her so quickly. She wondered what had made him suspicious. She had probably betrayed herself at the gate and he had analysed it on the ride up the trail. It would not need much to start him thinking for he missed very little of what happened around him. The stop had been to test his analysis and he now knew that her mood had changed.

It was almost noon when they reached the mine, despite Drew pushing the pace all morning. He dealt with the horses first, rubbing them down and picketing them on good graze. Then he set up a comfortable little camp under an overhanging rock, well back from the creek bank and clear of the water paths of the bush animals. He had apparently used the site many times, for there was a stone fireplace built against the rock face.

Given his description of what had happened to the overhang on the slope, Cynthia eyed the rock above her with some nervousness. He saw her glance and dryly assured her there was nothing to worry about with this overhang. They were well clear of the fault zone and the earth tremors never reached this far.

The primus stove was soon hissing busily as it heated the water for their tea and he set out the light lunch Dulcie had packed on the makeshift stone table to one side of the fireplace. His bustle filled the silence that was growing rapidly uncomfortable and Cynthia felt lost. Her resolve of the morning had lost its clarity and she would have done anything to return to the way that she had felt when she first woke.

As soon as lunch was finished—a meal filled with silences, he unpacked two modern miner's helmets; they were fitted with headlamps and waist pack batteries. Two powerful hand lanterns, a small sample bag and a geologist's rock hammer were the final additions.

It was time for them to enter the mine.

He led the way along the creek, across a patch of open ground and through a thin screen of bushes to an overhung path at the foot of the four-metre high creek bank.

'Does this look familiar?' he asked, turning back to her from a stout wooden door set into the entrance to the mine. Two solid pillars, set in concrete, held it in place. 'They replaced the original and strengthened it to stop hikers wandering about in the diggings,' Drew explained, taking a key from his pocket and unlocking the modern padlock that held it securely closed.

Cynthia looked around, trying to fit her memories of what she saw that night into what she could now see. They fitted very well, but then she would expect them to. He would not show her anything that clashed with what he expected her to remember. If she were to trap him, it would be with something that he did not know she had seen—some detail lodged in her almost photographic visual recall.

'It will be quicker if you describe what it is you remember of that night. I know the mine rather well. I spent a lot of time exploring it when I was young and believed that Andrew had left a secret here.'

183

He seemed unwilling to bring her suspicions out into the open, to acknowledge that she believed he already knew all the details. She was now equally reluctant to challenge his position and found herself describing in detail everything she remembered. He listened carefully, nodding occasionally at the recognition of some described feature.

'Alright,' he said, as she finished her description of their departure for the Chalet. 'I think I have it clearly in my mind. I'll lead off. Stop me if it becomes unfamiliar.'

He opened the door fully and waved her through, then turned back and locked the padlock on the inside.

'This will tell the Alpine Parks people we are inside and stop any wanderers from following us.'

He put the key on a ledge concealed from the doorway, making sure that she saw where it was.

'It would be embarrassing to lose it,' he said with a slight smile—the first he had allowed himself since their pause on the rock.

Switching on all four lamps banished the darkness and showed the mine tunnel leading away from them. There was a slight slope upwards and, although the tunnel was low, it was not so low that she could not walk upright.

The first thing she noticed was the trolley rails along the floor of the tunnel. They had corroded away until they were almost knife-edged. No trolley could have rolled along them in many years. Along one wall was a drain channel, a small trickle of water making its way to the outside world. She said nothing, just followed in his footsteps, occasionally stumbling over the piles of debris fallen from behind the age-weakened roof props. It did not feel very safe and she was conscious of the mass of rock above their heads.

Drew paused now and then to examine the wall or ceiling, but otherwise seemed unconcerned. All she could do was trust his superior knowledge.

The silence pressed in on her, making the sounds of their footsteps unnaturally loud. That was familiar. She had not remembered it till now, but she recalled how loud the odd sounds had seemed on that night and nodded in confirmation. Drew did not see her, but it didn't matter. It was not for him.

They reached an area where the tunnel widened. The roof rose above them and disappeared into the darkness of a vertical shaft.

'One of the vents Andrew mentioned,' Drew explained. 'It doglegs back towards the slope and comes out much higher. They are all fitted with steel grills these days. In the days when the mine was working, they would have been open.'

Three tunnels radiated out of the chamber and there was a shaft sunk in one corner. Drew led the way to it and shone his torch down to show the black surface of water lapping at its edges. It was the source of the trickle of water in the drain channel.

'All of the lower workings flood after the winter. It drains away during the summer, but they are never completely clear.'

'How did they dig them?'

'Hand pumping. You can see the channel along one side of the tunnel. It flowed out of there into the creek.'

A motorised pump would make short work of it, she thought. No one would hear the engine down here and the vent would take away the fumes. She filed the thought away for later consideration.

'That tunnel over there comes out high on the mountain. It fits your description of the way you left the mine. They dug it in the twenties to get rid of the spoil when they extended the diggings. We can check that first. It will save doubling back on the way out.'

There was now a sharp edge to his voice. It was curt, businesslike, almost as if he were engaged in a task that had become distasteful and wanted it done as soon as possible. He senses defeat, she thought, and wondered why she felt no triumph.

There was nothing familiar, or significant, in the tunnel they followed. The soft iron rails along the floor had corroded into uselessness and were buried in places by the dirt sifted down from the ceiling. Nothing seemed familiar until they reached the cave at the exit.

Enough daylight came in through the barred opening that they could switch off the lamps and the half light was closer to the illumination of an old-fashioned miner's lamp. It was achingly familiar. She could see exactly where Andrew had stepped into his skis, steadying himself against a convenient outcropping in the wall, only the missing winch and the solid black bars of steel set solidly into concrete clashed with her memory. Yet the latter looked as if they had been there for years. She walked over and grasped one. It felt as if it were rooted in the bedrock of the mountain itself.

'They put them in fifteen years ago,' Drew said. 'A group of hikers found the entrance and went down to explore. They vandalised everything they found, then one fool fell down the shaft and the Vic-Parks people had to come and rescue him. I think I would have left him until the mine flooded in the spring and drowned him.'

There was open anger in his voice, as if the hiker had vandalised a family tomb. Which was not that far from the truth, she thought.

She examined the concrete winch footing closely enough to see that they had removed the winch many years ago. The iron securing bolts were thinned by rust and useless. She stood up again and turned to him.

'Where is the wooden cabin?'

His eyes held hers for a moment, but he made no reply. He merely turned away and led the way back into the mine, switching on his headlamp and hand lantern as he went. She switched on her own lights and followed.

They reached the vent chamber and took the left-hand tunnel. It seemed to lead directly up into the mountain.

There was less debris in this tunnel. It seemed carved out of solid rock, needing little or no support from the wooden props. The ceiling was higher. The walls cut with niches for storage at regular intervals. The iron rails on the floor were in better condition, less corroded. The air was drier and there was no seepage from the walls. The lack of dampness made it feel warmer. It was a logical place to build living quarters.

Ten metres further and they reached another vent chamber; this one cut entirely from living rock. The remains of a stone chimney ran up one side of the vent, half blocking the entrance to the blind end of the tunnel beyond. There, she could see the ruins of the wooden cabin. The vandalism was shockingly complete, yet it could not disguise the scene from the memory of her backward glance as she had left the cabin following Andrew.

They had smashed down the front wall and the dividing wall behind it. The stove was now a sagging, broken thing and, opposite it, the table kneeled drunkenly on broken legs. She pushed past it into the second room, the light from the lanterns revealing in cruel detail the damage done to her refuge. The pot-bellied stove was a scatter of broken cast iron. The bunk gaped with smashed sides and the armchair was a splintered heap. It was cruel. She felt personally affronted, for everything was eerily familiar. She could feel Andrew's anger across the years that separated them.

Something rolled under her foot, nearly sending her into the remains of the bunk. She looked down, her headlamp following the direction of her eyes, just in time to see something disappear between two gaping floorboards. She knelt down to retrieve it and came to her feet with a battered chess piece in her hand. It was her white king. Age had stripped the polish of loving use, but the crack in the crown remained. She dug the dirt from it with her thumbnail as she stood by the ruined bunk, looking around in disbelief.

It was utterly impossible. Three months ago, she had played chess in this room. Andrew had warmed his feet at that pot-bellied stove while he had waited for her to wake. She looked up. The light from her headlamp centred on a hand-carved insignia and she recognised it, both from the cap badge and from her memory of the first time she woke. The cuts were no longer new and a split in the wood made it difficult to read the numerals of the Twenty-Fourth Regiment of Foot's crest, but it still fitted precisely the picture from her mind.

She looked down at the white king and slowly closed her fingers around it in a fist. They tightened until she was grasping the chess piece as if it were her last hold on reality. A terrible sense of loss flooded her mind. She had killed Andrew Mitchell completely, consigning him forever to the land of the dead by the proof that he was a ghost. The cabin felt suddenly empty, as if a familiar presence had just left.

She did not know when she started crying. The tears appeared without warning, dribbling down her cheeks and dropping silently to the ancient dust at her feet. She switched off the hand lantern and closed her eyes. She did not want to see any more.

Drew was gentleness itself. He came up and put his arms around her. She turned and rested her head on his shoulder. He stood there patiently, doing nothing more than hold her, until the tears ceased of their own accord.

There was no longer any purpose in their presence, so they left the now deserted cabin.

She felt numb, following Drew as if she were a little child as he retraced their steps. It was already early evening when they emerged from the mine. A fact Cynthia noted without interest, for she felt exhausted and the long grass dragged at her feet as she walked. She saw nothing of the scenery. She just followed silently in Drew's footsteps, her mind unwilling to come to terms with what had happened. Of one thing she was certain, just being around Drew Mitchell would daunt the strongest.

Everything kept changing. The certainties of one moment became the doubts of the next. Now, she suspected that it was all gone beyond recall, leaving only a feeling of awkwardness between them that frightened her. It felt like a chasm deeper than she could ever bridge.

When they reached their camp, Drew set up her swag against the rock wall, half folded to make a comfortable couch. She sank onto it and sat there in a daze, her arms wrapped around her knees, as he built a fire. She felt totally chilled and was grateful for the promise of warmth. A thousand thoughts jostled for her attention, but her brain would admit none of them. It abandoned itself to what she had felt in that rock bound cabin.

Andrew Mitchell had been there. His presence had filled the space. There had been no doubt in her mind. Then she had felt him leave and all that remained was a terrible sense of loss. The High Plains Ghost was no more. There was nothing in her understanding of how the world worked that would explain what she felt in the mine, yet it had an aching clarity that she could not deny. She felt lost.

10

'Did your private inquiry people ever find out how the Mitchell men became besotted with blondes?' Drew asked, not looking up from his task of packing away the last plate.

Their meal was over. He had served a hot wholesome stew, obviously a favourite of the Mitchell males, complete with fresh bread and topped off by tinned fruit. Drew had done everything. They now sat on their swags, only an arm's length apart, facing the warmth of the fire. Drew had the packsaddle between his knees.

'No,' Cynthia said, lifting her gaze from the coals and turning to face him.

It was the first time since their return from the mine that he had offered anything beyond strictly necessary conversation.

'It is in the seventh journal, after Rorke's Drift. Andrew had gone out with the others to collect the weapons from the dead Zulus and he came across a dying Induna—a field commander in the Zulu army.

' "Bayete, Great One," the Zulu greeted him, using the royal salute to show his respect. "You have come to ease my pain and send me to join the others."

'The Zulus usually dispatched their badly wounded warriors, both to prevent suffering

192

and as a mark of respect.

'Andrew examined the Zulu. It was obvious that the man could not live long. He did what he could to make him comfortable, though it was not much. He had just rocked back on his heels to consider the matter when the Zulu spoke again. "I saw you from the hillside. Your rifle rolled like the thunder on the plains when the storms come and our men fell like dry corn before you. It will be an honour to die at your hand."

'The rapid fire Henry rifle must have made an impression when compared to the single shot Martini-Henry military rifles.

'The Zulu closed his eyes for a while and then opened them again.

'"Ah, you have brought the others of your tribe. The shadowy men I saw at your shoulder."

'Andrew looked around, but there was no one there. It seemed pointless to contradict the dying man, so he said nothing.

'"Even your Great Elephant has come . . . and the daughter of the Sun stands at his shield arm. The glow of her hair blinds my eyes."

'Andrew looked around again, expecting to see John Chard, the officer in command, but they were still alone.

'"Bayete," the Zulu saluted someone only he could see and the pain flowed out of his face. "The golden-haired one has enough

193

mercy for all. She will be the mother of a great tribe and rule over the land owned by her sons. They will all be men of men, as their fathers are before them." '

'Then he died.'

Drew reached out and prodded the fire with the steel hobble post.

'Andrew interpreted it that one of the Mitchell men would marry a blonde and live happily ever after on Mitchell's Run,' he said wryly. 'He didn't entirely believe it, but we've had a preponderance of blonde women marry into the family over the years.'

'What's the Great Elephant?'

'It was the Zulu name for Shaka, the Great Chief. Others have tried to claim it since, but never quite made it.'

'What about Goldilocks?'

'Andrew brought back an original edition of the fairy tales collected by the Brothers Grimm. We still read it to the Mitchell children. The story of Goldilocks and the Three Bears is a little different to the modern version. In this version, the three bears are respected forest dwellers and Goldilocks is the spoilt child of the local dignitary. The baby bear recognises that she is just lonely and did not intend any harm. He runs after her to say that he forgives her and will play with her. I have always assumed that the name came from that. Andrew always read it to his brother's children. If you link it to the Induna's prophecy, it makes sense. I know that the woodcut illustration of Goldilocks makes her a real beauty and has the sun haloing her hair.'

Cynthia turned her eyes back to the coals. Her mind raced. She had to find a way to use the moment. He had made the first move. It was up to her now. However, he continued before she could think of anything.

'I love this country.' His voice was musing, as if he were thinking aloud. 'It always draws me back. I would find it hard to leave for good.'

She nodded uncertainly, not understanding where he was leading.

'The first time I rode up into these mountains with Andrew's journals in my saddlebags, I felt very special. I was the continuation of a line and I knew exactly what it was that I wanted. Nothing seemed quite so important as to finish the task he had started.'

He paused, and looked directly at her for the first time since they had emerged from the mine.

'There were benefits to it. Anything that I wanted to do for that purpose had the immediate approval of the family. At family gatherings, I was the noted man. They respected my opinions, accepted my decisions without quibble. It was heady wine and I drank it willingly. My path lay clearly defined.'

He got up and added wood to the fire, prodding it with the picket pin until he was satisfied.

'Then you appeared on the scene.' He put down the picket pin quite deliberately and turned back to her. 'I could not believe that anything quite so beautiful could exist. That first night, when we dined together, I felt gauche and awkward, like a teenager on his first date.'

'You certainly didn't appear that way,' she said, making her first tentative contribution and praying that it was not a misstep. 'At the lake, you put me in my place quite thoroughly. I had never had anyone walk away from me before.'

Her words raised a slight smile.

'I can understand that,' he agreed. 'It was the first time I had ever resented Andrew. You were there because of him. I meant nothing to you. I only held your attention by talking of him.'

It was amazing how differently they had seen that evening. She had to fight down the surge of hope. She still had no idea where this was leading, yet Drew did nothing without a purpose.

'The more I learnt about you, the more my admiration grew. Still, it should not have surprised me. You came well recommended.' He saw her puzzlement and smiled. 'No one is quite sure what happens when Andrew rescues some one. He seems to be able to bend all the rules, as we understand them, but there are some common features. You have to be very near death when he first appears. Every rescue apparently has to begin at the exact moment you have given up and begun the process of dying. A second feature, that is not so immediately apparent, is that every person he has rescued has gone on to do something of value. The girl from a couple of years ago recently announced an important discovery in cancer research. Only the three who extended the mine do not have obvious achievements. I thought at first that the extension of the mine was their purpose and I explored it very thoroughly, but there's nothing there.'

'Was she a blonde too? The girl he rescued,' Cynthia asked; she had automatically assumed that she was.

Drew laughed. The serious expression on his face replaced by a reminiscing smile. 'No. She was a mousy brunette, thick glasses and bad teeth, but she hunted me down none the less. I had to disappear into the bush for a while.'

'Did you walk out on her too?'

'It would have been too cruel. She had none of your advantages. Her self-esteem was rather fragile.'

'That makes me sound a little vain.'

'Aren't you?'

This was the Drew Mitchell of old. Whatever it was that was bothering him, it had not blunted the sharpness of his tongue. She did not mind. As long as he kept talking to her, she would allow him any liberty.

'When I got back to Mansfield and found that Beth had posted the invitations, I gave her such a hug that she thought I would break her ribs. It gave me the excuse to ring you.'

Cynthia nodded thoughtfully. She had been right. It had taken something greater than his pride to make that telephone call, but it had not been greed. The whole Mitchell family was used to Andrew's rescues. They had a well-tuned plan to deal with the reactions of the rescued, except that this time one of them had become involved personally. The others, who knew Drew so much better than her, had recognised it immediately and obviously approved. Dulcie and Beth's actions now made perfect sense. They had been welcoming her to the clan.

'I don't know what you felt in the mine,' Drew continued. 'It was obviously very strong. What I felt was a sense of completion.' His expression was serious once more, the moment of lightness behind him. 'Andrew had finished whatever he stayed behind to do. I could feel him leave. My problem is that I do not know what it is that he's finished. There still so much left undone.'

'Maybe it was to bring us together?'

'If that is so, then we have a long way to go.'

'Why? Did last night mean nothing to you?' she asked, surprise making her voice sound unintentionally sharp, almost shrewish.

'Apparently more than it meant to you this morning.'

'I became afraid of the future,' she explained, softening her voice to make amends for her earlier tone. 'I am not as strong as my mother. I could never let you go off to Africa.'

He looked at her sharply, then retreated to his observer mode while he apparently adjusted his perceptions to a new piece of information.

'I guess we both have our problems,' he agreed thoughtfully. 'I thought you were still afraid that I was after your father's money. I have seen the idea in your face once or twice.' Cynthia flushed. Surely, she was not that obvious. 'Yet that is nothing against the real problem for me, particularly after seeing your reaction in the mine,' he continued. 'I will never be completely sure that you love me, and not Andrew's shadow.'

It was out in the open. In an instant, she saw how galling it had become for him, trapped in another man's shade. Andrew was the measure of everything that he did. No wonder he had been desperate to succeed. Only then would he stand in the full sunlight as his own man. As the younger brother, Andrew would have understood perfectly.

She was uncomfortably aware that she had just unconsciously perpetuated the problem by thinking about it in terms of Andrew's reaction. This was not going to be easy. It was all unfamiliar territory to her, yet it was clear that she would only get the one chance. A single mistake would destroy everything.

Drew himself was the problem. He had surrendered so completely to the legend that there was nothing that was not a reflection of his ancestor. Even his flying was merely an extension of Andrew's riding skill. Only now did she understand how powerfully she had affected him by declaring him 'a unique individual' in his studio. She had to find another way to reach out and touch him, but her mind was a blank. Honesty seemed her only resource.

'I can't deny any of the things you have said,' she began. 'I could not believe in a ghost and the feelings you created frightened me. They were totally beyond anything I had ever known and I could not control them. The belief that you were hiding an illegal mine protected me from them. It gave me an escape clause.'

She paused to study his face, trying to read his response. He was evaluating her words, weighing them against her actions.

Encouraged, she continued. 'I will always be grateful to Andrew, he brought us together, but I fell in love with you. I can't tell you what caused it, or list the qualities that are uniquely yours. I only know that I do not want to lose you. If you wanted Sheldon money for

Mitchell's Run, my father would give it to you, but I know you better than that. You will do it on your own terms, or not at all. You are too much your own man. As for my fear of the future, the sense of loss that I felt when Andrew left, has made me fear losing you even more than being left alone.'

She stopped. Her last card was on the table. It was his call.

'Can I have that in writing?' he asked, a crooked smile emerging as he spoke.

Her world was born anew. It glowed around her. She flung herself into his arms with a violence that toppled them onto his back and almost into the fire. She did not care. Nothing could go wrong now.

They made love. They lay in each other's arms and talked happy nonsense. They kissed. No one else existed. Theirs was a world without a past, without a future. There was only this moment, this now. Cynthia had never known such unfettered happiness.

'So this is what all the fuss was about,' Drew said, as they lay with their bodies still fused together after the act of love.

The mischief in his voice forewarned her, but she fell in with his scheme anyway.

'All right,' she said. 'I'll be your straight man and ask "what".'

'I don't think that anyone would agree that you were either straight or a man,' he argued, running his hands over the curve of her buttocks to emphasise his point. 'I think the churches make a mistake when they make it sound so tempting,' he continued, returning to his original thought. 'I could become quite fond of living in Cyn.'

It took a moment for the pun to sink in and she greeted it with the groan that good puns always elicit before threatening with physical violence should he ever repeat it. In her heart, she knew that the threat was futile. That type of joke lives forever in a marriage and she was happily contemplating the prospect.

It was late when Drew decided that he must check the horses. She had to stifle a smile at the sight of him, naked except for his boots, as he walked away from the campsite. She winced a little as she rolled onto her back. Although he had laid one swag on top of the other, the padding was still a little thin and the ground exceedingly hard. It was a very small price to pay, but she suspected that the ride back to Mitchell's Run would not be entirely comfortable.

He came back, built up the fire for the night and warmed himself at it before joining her in the swag. They wrestled happily as she tried to avoid contact with the chilled flesh that the fire had not reached. He was merciless.

'Think of it as your duty,' he advised running a cold palm down the centre of her lower back and enjoying the resultant thrust against him as she tried to avoid it.

'I'll make you sleep on your own,' she threatened.

'Will you?' he challenged.

'No,' she admitted, seeking his lips with her own and allowing the distraction to anaesthetise her against the contact of his chilled flesh. That was only the beginning . . .

Midnight was a distant memory and the Southern Cross had long turned over, yet they were still awake. She should have been tired, but she was not. She wanted the night to go on forever, happy to greet the new day still awake and still locked in her lover's embrace. Drew seemed content to let her have her way, smiling at her nonsense, gently caressing her body with his hands, while his lips touched places grown so sensitive to him that she moaned softly in response.

When he rolled over to feed the fire a second time, she relented.

'We should get some sleep,' she said tentatively, as if half hoping that he would disagree.

'It would be wise,' he agreed, laughter lines crinkling the skin at the outer corners of his eyes.

She demanded a final kiss and then allowed him to turn her so that she faced the fire, her back fitting into the curve of his body. His left arm lay across her body with his hand resting on hers outside the blanket. She could see the auburn tint in the hairs on his wrist.

'A proper gentleman,' she said, suddenly drowsy. 'You remembered to take off your watch.'

He chuckled, but made no reply.

Now that she had surrendered to it, sleep was rushing towards her like a wave of darkness. It had almost overwhelmed her when her mind screamed alarm and she started awake, her body jerking with the shock.

'What's up?' Drew asked, immediately alert.

Her mind was racing.

'Nothing! . . . It was nothing. I was just on the edge of sleep and thought that I saw something. Obviously, I was mistaken,' she explained, half-truthfully. 'Go to sleep. Morning will come too early as it is.'

He grunted doubtfully, but lay back and she had to wait a long time before she felt him relax in sleep. She forced herself to lie quietly until she was sure, and then lifted her head enough to examine his wrist.

The pale shadow of a watchband on a tanned wrist was innocuous enough. She had probably seen the same thing a hundred times or more. She had even seen it on the wrist of the man who had pretended to be Andrew Mitchell in the mountain mine. He had unwittingly shown it to her when he arranged her bed covers the first time that she woke. It had not consciously registered at the time, just lain dormant in her visual memory until the trigger came.

How she wished that it had not!

*   *   *

It felt as if she had no sooner closed her eyes than he woke her with a steaming mug of tea. She tried to be gracious, but it was a dismal failure. He just grinned at her and went off to bring in the horses. They would have to be on their way quite smartly, he explained, if she was to see her father at the airport. She wrapped a blanket around her shoulders and sat cross-legged on the sleeping swag, sipping the hot liquid and coming to terms with the day.

There would be no dramatic confrontation. Perhaps they had invented wristwatches by 1886. Perhaps Andrew wore a wrist guard. She did not know. She was not even sure that she wanted to find out. The whole thing had become a conflict of impossibilities that hours of sleepless thought had done nothing to resolve.

Nothing could change the certainty she had felt in the mine. The ruined cabin had been her place of refuge. That it had been vandalised fifteen years before did not change that. It probably meant that she spent time in Andrew's world, wherever that might be. When everything is impossible, every impossibility therefore becomes credible.

She shook her head tiredly. It was all

beyond her for the moment.

Drew came back with the horses and gave each a measured amount of feed. They nuzzled him, competing more for his attention than for the feed. They loved him, particularly the mare. Cynthia joked feebly with him about it and he responded with such relaxed happiness that her spirits lifted.

He did not realise that anything had happened and it was important to her that he remain in ignorance. She would have to resolve this issue herself. No more scatter-brained accusations. Now that she knew how vulnerable he was, she had the responsibility for his happiness as well as her own. It was the one resolution she had reached in the pre-dawn hours of wakefulness. It would not be easy. He had demonstrated that yesterday.

She forced herself to smile and let her hand linger on his arm. His pleased grin made it easier and she soon found that there was little need for pretence in her reaction to his presence. Her body had no doubts and it was simply a case of letting it take control. She rose to her feet and dressed, changing her underwear but retaining the clothes she had worn yesterday. She would shower and change at Mitchell's Run before they left. Her hair, she simply pulled into a ponytail, secured by an elastic hair tie. It was low enough that the Akubra hat sat comfortably on her head.

Drew stopped to admire her before he

rigged the packsaddle on Ginger and cleared the camp. Everything that did not disappear into the two panniers, he lashed securely to the crosstrees. Saddling the horses seemed a simple chore by comparison, one he carried out with the economy of effort that came from years of practice. She could only watch and admire, consoling herself that they were saving time by her not being involved.

The previous day's ride and their exertions since had woken muscles normally unused. She was not actively uncomfortable yet, but she hoped that the ride back would be at an easier pace.

He seemed to read her thoughts, beginning slowly and building the pace so gradually that she hardly noticed it. They rode side by side for most of the way, falling into line only when the trail became too narrow. The gradual stretching of her muscles went almost painlessly and other thoughts occupied her mind, diverting it from the clash of her beliefs and the evidence of her eyes.

It was just as well. The certainties in the mine were fading and another odd flash of visual memory supported the evidence of her eyes. This one was of Andrew's painting of Rorke's Drift. His left wrist was clearly visible as he held the fore-grip of the Henry rifle and it was bare. The rest of the painting was so detailed that he would not have omitted a watch or wristband.

They reached the top of the cliff above Mitchell's Run late in the morning. Drew motioned her to take the lead and the mare responded willingly, entering the narrow gap in the rock that marked the entrance to the fissure. They negotiated it without a problem, though riding down was harder than riding up, and then skirted the foot of the cliff. They paused at the end of the first traverse of the zigzag trail while Drew checked the harnesses. With the weight thrown forward, some of the straps needed tightening. Once he was satisfied, they continued their ride to Mitchell's Run.

The first tremor was so slight that she thought she imagined it. It came when they were in the narrowest part of the trail, midway across the slope, and all she could do was twist in the saddle and look back at Drew. His head was up and he was looking around alertly, obviously he had noticed it too. He made her pause when they reached the end of that traverse and sat in the saddle considering their position. The trail led once more across the full face of the slope, then reversed itself and came mid way back to the gate. They waited for ten minutes, but there were no more tremors.

'There has been a small amount of seismic activity building up for a while. I checked it on the Internet before we left. That may have been the result. The subsidence due to the prolonged drought is adding to the tectonic plate pressure in this area.'

Cynthia recognised that only half his mind was on his words. The unexplained technical terms were just the surface indications of his thoughts. He obviously considered there was a serious risk, otherwise he would have said nothing, just as he did in the mine.

'Lead out,' he instructed. 'Stop when you reach the other side.' His tone brooked no discussion. 'The trees thin out below that point. We'll ride directly down the slope and not risk another transit to the gate. I would go straight down now, but the scrub is too thick.'

The mare started uncertainly, her rider's apprehension transmitted through the reins. The other two horses fell into line, the gelding immediately behind the mare and old Ginger plodding phlegmatically behind. Nothing happened in the first fifty metres and the mare settled down enough to allow Cynthia to glance back at Drew.

He was standing in the stirrups, his head just above the level of the surrounding scrub, looking uphill.

At that moment, the first major tremor struck. The mare squealed and went to her knees, almost unseating her rider. She scrambled back to her feet and Cynthia could do little more than cling to the saddle, all control of the horse lost. Behind her the gelding snorted nervously but the firm hand at the reins steadied him and he did no more than stamp his iron-shod feet.

At the second tremor, the mare went berserk, rearing to rid herself of her encumbrance. She pivoted on her hind legs, turning to face back the way they had come. Her forelegs came down with a crash that jarred through her body, jerking Cynthia forward and almost out of the saddle. At that moment, Drew drove the gelding forward, shouldering the mare off the trail while he grasped Cynthia's waist and lifted her clear of the saddle. She felt his arm around her and let go, her arms reaching for his neck. From above, she heard an ominous rumble.

'Swing your leg across behind me,' Drew said urgently, twisting in the saddle to aid her movement.

There was a moment of confusion, when her arms and legs seemed tangled and unco-operative, then it all seemed to sort itself out and she was astride the gelding behind Drew with her arms locked about his waist. Drew barely waited until she settled before he drove the gelding forward, lifting the horse to a full gallop along the narrow trail. An unexplained wind bent the light scrub downhill and buffeted the gelding and its passengers while the rumble had grown to a roar that shook the ground.

With nothing to do but hold on, Cynthia's mind provided an explanation for the wind. It was displaced air. The mass of rock above them had started to fall and was accelerating, pushing ahead of it the lighter air. This would lift dust and small stones, followed by heavier stones and then the mass of the rockslide itself. Their only hope was to ride clear of its path and she would be able to tell how close it was by the size of the stones. It was not a comforting thought.

Twice the gelding stumbled, but Drew seemed to lift him up by sheer will and brute strength. Earth and small stones flew in the wind. Cynthia felt a larger one strike painfully in the small of her back as the wind increased in intensity. Another, even larger, swept the Akubra from her head, the glancing blow driving her head forward against Drew and making it ring. Fortunately, the stiffened felt of the hat brim and her ponytail absorbed some of the impact, or it would have knocked her from the horse. Dust stung her eyes and she could barely see the trail ahead. The end of the traverse loomed in front of them, a thick stand of trees beyond it, but Drew did not draw rein. Instead, he drove the gelding towards a narrow gap between two trees at its lower edge. Cynthia hunched herself against the impact, tightening her grip around his waist, but they cleared both trees and were through with only the painful whip of light branches to show for it. Behind her, she heard the mare scream in agony, the sound cutting through the roar of the rockslide.

Drew let the gelding slide to a halt on its haunches before they struck the next stand of trees. They were now clear of the rockslide. The gelding recovered its feet and stood on trembling legs as Drew lowered Cynthia to the ground, then dismounted. Behind them, the mare's screams went on and on, making it obvious that she was badly injured.

'Hold the reins,' he said, handing her the reins, but it was more as a distraction than from any need. The gelding was totally blown from carrying the double burden at such a pace. It could do nothing but stand on trembling legs with its head down. 'I'll check on the mare.' He went back into the dust cloud that obscured the whole slope behind them and she could do nothing but wait until the mare's screams ended abruptly in the sound of a sickening crunch of bone. In the relative silence that followed, she could hear the sound of her own sobbing breath and the wheezing of the gelding beside her. Everything else was still, shocked into silence by the violence that had preceded it. The terror of clinging helplessly to Drew as he saved them subsided very slowly and she felt physically ill.

The dust cloud had thinned markedly before Drew returned and his appearance gave her some hint of how she must look herself. He had lost his hat in the wind and dust had turned his hair a mousy brown. It had also thickened his eyelashes so they stood out darkly against the patina of brown that hid his skin. There was a cut on his cheek from a flying stone and the blood had mixed with the dust in a dark crust below it.

She took a step, intending to cross the distance between them. Instead, she sank to her knees and then collapsed into a sitting position. The minutes of waiting after he had silenced the mare had completely drained her of the will to remain upright.

He reached her before she could sink further and scooped her up in his arms. 'Are you hurt?' he demanded.

'No,' she said. 'Just terribly frightened. I was all right until the mare stopped screaming, but, after that, I worried that there might be another slide and I would lose you.'

'That is not such a silly idea,' he agreed. 'There is always the chance of aftershocks and there is no telling how stable the remainder of the cliff face is now. As soon as you are able, we should move further away. I only stopped to make sure Ginger was beyond any aid.'

'He's dead?'

'Yes.' Drew did not go into details.

The gelding had recovered enough to nuzzle Drew's shoulder.

'There you go, boy,' Drew said comfortingly and patted the horse's cheek. 'We all made it. Do you think that you can carry my pretty lady back to the homestead?'

The horse blew softly through his nostrils and seemed to nod his head in agreement, so Drew lifted her into the saddle and let her sit there while he checked the horse's legs for damage. Once he was satisfied, he took the reins in his hand then started off on foot, leading the gelding. Cynthia clung to the saddlebow and submitted to the arrangement. She did not turn to look at the devastation. She just watched Drew lead the way between the trees out into the cleared area.

It was not until they broke clear of the trees that she saw how massive the slide had been. Fifty metres of the fence was missing, either buried or swept away by a jumbled mass of rock, earth and shattered vegetation that reached twice that distance into the open paddock.

The dust had now settled enough that she could see the changed face of the cliff at the top of the escarpment. The whole of the jutting parapet had disappeared and a bright new rock-face stood at the head of the slope, a triangle of torn earth pointing at it.

Cynthia saw the sudden tension in Drew's body as he looked upwards.

'At the base of the cliff,' he said. 'Look at the base. It looks like a mine tunnel dug straight into the cliff. I cannot believe Andrew could have been that desperate.' There was admiration, rather than doubt, in his tone. He already knew the lengths Andrew would go to to save Mitchell's Run.

She could see how much he wanted to climb the slope, only his concern for her was holding him back.

'We are quite close,' she said. 'I won't be afraid as long as we are together.'

'There should be a period of grace before any aftershocks arrive,' he said thoughtfully. 'Are you sure that you're all right?'

'I came up here to look at Andrew's mine,' she said. 'It seems we were looking in the wrong place after all.'

Drew looked at her for a long moment, his eyes unreadable. He had heard something in her voice that disturbed him enough to turn his attention from the mine. It appeared to make his decision for him and he turned away and started leading the gelding up the slope.

The horse began reluctantly but soon needed no urging, following Drew as willingly as a favourite dog. Cynthia kept her grip on the saddlebow. She no longer felt totally confident of her riding ability and the blow to her head must have been more serious than she thought. Her vision kept blurring momentarily and she had a throbbing headache.

It took them ten minutes of scrambling to reach the mine entrance.

There was a small level area immediately in front, where the overhang had rested before it toppled down the hill. It was large enough for the gelding to stand comfortably and Drew lifted her down from the saddle. Looking down into the valley, she could see the battered 4WD parked beyond the fan of torn vegetation and earth. Jack and Peter were already a third of the way up the slope towards them. Drew raised his arm in acknowledgment of Jack's shout.

'Well, let's have a look,' Drew said, taking a small hand torch from the gelding's saddlebags.

This was much different from the mountain mine. There were no props, only a rough irregularly shaped tunnel under a strata of rock. It was not even straight, curving away to their left.

They found what was left of Andrew Mitchell half propped against the far wall. A dried collection of bones discoloured by lichen with a tree root passing through the gaping eye socket before disappearing back into the earth. A familiar large belt buckle lay in the area of the midriff and a rusting colt revolver with discoloured bone butt plates to one side. What identified him was the journal lying across the leg bones. It had been attacked by lichen as well, but was in surprisingly good condition.

Cynthia stooped to pick it up, but Drew stopped her.

'Don't touch anything,' he said sharply. 'The State Coroner will be involved. I do not want anything to compromise our claim.'

Startled, she turned to look at him. He was looking beyond Andrew Mitchell at the broad band of gold bearing quartz that took up most of the end wall. Thick veins of gold gleamed in the light.

Cynthia was slowly emerging from the passivity of shock. To this point, her mind had worked slowly, if at all. She had observed what was happening around her from a distance. Even her own actions had appeared as those of another person. Suddenly, all the events of the last twenty-four hours rushed in on her and she began to shake. Drew immediately forgot everything but her. He held her in his arms while her body shook uncontrollably. She surrendered to his embrace, looking over his shoulder at the remains of Andrew Mitchell, still lit by the reflected light from the torch in Drew's hand.

'At least you will be able to stop pretending to be him,' she said, her tone matter of fact.

She felt Drew's body stiffen, but he said nothing.

Oddly, this infuriated her and all her bottled up doubts poured out as accusations. She forgot the certainties of the mountain mine. Nothing mattered but his betrayal of her trust. She thrust herself out of his arms and stood swaying uncertainly.

'I know it was you in the mine,' she said. 'You took off your watch, but you forgot to darken the area that it covers. I saw it the night you rescued me and again last night. Nothing matters to you beyond Mitchell's Run.'

Her voice grew ragged with the pain of her thoughts and pound of her pulse in the pool of pain that was the back of her head.

'Everything that you have said to me is a lie, no matter how cleverly disguised. I will never be able to trust you.'

Drew said nothing. He just stood there with his arms hanging loosely by his sides, his palms towards her in a vaguely pleading position.

'You should never have changed your name,' she continued. 'Drew Mitchell is just a figment of Andrew's imagination.'

It took another earth tremor to stop her. She froze in fear; dimly aware of Jack's startled shout echoing in the tunnel. Drew's white, shocked face was all she could see as her head seemed to explode in pain and she fell away from him into a deep well of blackness. His voice accompanied her. He had finally answered her . . .

'Damn you, Andrew!' he said. 'Will you never let me go.' His pain tore at her heart, but it was too late.

11

'Hello, there,' Dulcie said. 'You've decided to join us again.'

Cynthia looked at her blankly, totally disoriented. She did not even react when a stranger's face replaced Dulcie.

'Don't try to move,' he said. 'There is a helicopter waiting outside and you are strapped into a stretcher for transport to Melbourne. Both your parents are here and I will be coming with you. There is nothing to worry you. We are just playing safe after your collapse in the mine. I think it was more the effect of shock than physical injuries.'

It did not feel like shock. The whole back of her head ached as if some one had driven a spike through her skull at the top of her spine and her body felt as if it were a mass of bruises.

'Drew?' she asked painfully.

Dulcie's face replaced that of the stranger.

'He's all right,' she said. 'He's just gone up to the mine with Ted Hughes, the local police sergeant.'

Memory flooded back into Cynthia's mind and she closed her eyes to shut out the world. She had failed him again. Would she ever learn?

From her refuge, she listened to the bustle

as her mother fussed and her father established a rapport with both Dulcie and Jack. Peter came and went, at the disposal of everyone it seemed. She opened her eyes and he smiled at her uncertainly, not sure of how to treat her, or even if he should approach her. She remembered that with great shame later; he was the most innocent of them all.

The stranger, who turned out to be the local doctor, a young man not long out of his internship, consulted with the two paramedics of the helicopter crew and came back to kneel beside the stretcher.

'How do you feel?' he asked. 'I don't want to give you a shot of anything unless it is absolutely necessary. I will be with you all the way.'

Cynthia managed to nod, the movement more of her eyes than her head. 'I don't need anything,' she said uncertainly and the doctor surrendered her to the care of the paramedics as they carried her out to the helicopter and secured the stretcher in place.

Her parents and the doctor joined them and the helicopter lifted smoothly into the sky. Cynthia closed her eyes once more and drifted beyond the pain in her body and her mind.

The helicopter landed in the park opposite the hospital and the last she saw of the young country doctor was him talking to another white-coated doctor, while her father listened. She did not even have the chance to say goodbye. The hospital system had taken charge and it carried her away, as helpless as a child.

A battery of tests and a million questions later, she arrived in a private room, already filled with flowers. The male nurse, young and good-looking, fussed over her for a while before he administered an injection and left, drawing the blinds.

She woke to find her father sitting by the bed.

Alerted by the groan that she made as she found that her muscles protested against all movement, he rose to his feet and leant across to kiss her on the forehead. 'You gave us a bit of a fright, young lady,' he said. 'However, all the tests have been clear and they will let you go home in a day or two.' He took her hand and gave it a squeeze. 'I must leave now; my next flight is in three hours. I've been booked on every one since I cancelled.'

'Thanks, Dad.'

'It was not really necessary. You were in good hands. I just reacted to the thought of losing you.'

The familiar staccato certainties made her smile. 'You had better go,' she said. 'It is a long way to the airport.'

He smiled, blew her a kiss and then walked out.

She must have drifted off to sleep, for the next thing she was aware of was the male nurse taking her blood pressure and temperature.

'Hello,' she said groggily.

'Hello, yourself,' he replied, smiling brightly. 'We have more flowers than we can fit in this room. Would you mind if we shared them with one or two in the public ward?'

'Of course,' she agreed.

'I don't suppose that would include this one,' he said, holding up a vase in which stood one perfect red rose.

'The florist downstairs has instructions to supply one just like this, every morning that you are here.'

'Is there a note?'

No,' the nurse said. 'I have the feeling he didn't think one was necessary.'

'How do you know that it is a "he"?'

'Isn't it?'

She had no reply. She merely slipped down the bed and closed her eyes until she could just see him through the curtain of her lashes, pretending tiredness to curtail the conversation. He stood there smiling for a moment and then left the room.

As soon as she was certain that he was gone, she opened her eyes fully and studied the single bloom. It would be typical of Drew, she thought, remembering the rose he sent to her mother, but she could not believe that he had forgiven her so easily. Her subconscious mind had chosen its words well. They were the most wounding that it could use. For him simply to ignore them was unbelievable. It made her feel utterly low.

It had to be her father!

Their doctor came in to see her. He had been a part of their family for as long as she could remember. An ageless man, always immaculately suited, even in his consulting rooms, he had doctored her through childhood aliments, through puberty and all the other stages till now.

'You look a lot better now,' he began, picking up the observations chart from the foot of the bed. 'You had us all suspecting some degree of brain damage, your behaviour was so unusual.' He grinned at her, as he had done many times when she was younger. 'I told them that it wasn't possible. You don't have a brain. I've known that since you were a child.

'I think you just ran up against something more than you could handle and your mind took the easy way out. There are all sorts of modern names for it, but I saw it most of all amongst the troops. It is a build up. They can handle each individual shock, but if they come too rapidly, a part of their mind takes over and tries to create a refuge for them. That's what I think happened to you.'

He saw her looking at him doubtfully and laughed.

'Then again, I am just an old GP. What would I know about how a modern young woman reacts to a ghost and two near death experiences.'

He had checked her out after her experience in the snow and she had told him the whole story. He was that sort of doctor.

She smiled uncertainly.

'That's even better,' he said, an encouraging smile turning his face almost cherubic. 'I prescribe another day of bed rest, a week of thinking, while your mother fusses over you, and then, action. You will know what to do by then.'

Jeanette Sheldon was her next visitor.

'I have seen your father off,' she said. 'He gave me instructions right up to the point when he went through immigration. Now, Henry tells me you are coming home for a week and that I can cook as much chicken broth as I like for you. That man is quite crazy.' She said it all without taking a breath.

Cynthia realised abruptly that normally imperturbable Jeanette Sheldon was nervous. She had just farewelled a husband in whom she saw very real signs of age and she knew that where he was going would accelerate that process. The black wings of death had twice brushed her only child, raising the spectre of a lonely old age, which suddenly appeared to be just around the next corner. No wonder she found it difficult to manage and hid herself in inanity. These were the things normally kept beyond the boundaries of her strictly ordered life. A flash of memory told her that Drew had recognised her mother's need for order as what it was, a form of protection.

'Don't worry, Mum. I am sure that he will be all right.'

'You haven't called me that for many years.' Jeanette sat on the bed and took Cynthia's hand in hers. 'Are you going to be all right?' she asked.

'I ache in places that I didn't know existed and my subconscious has apparently driven away the man I love, but that is hardly a challenge to a Sheldon woman.'

'No, it is not. Now that you have recognised it,' Jeanette agreed. 'He struck me as the type of young man who looked far below the surface of everything.'

'You don't know how badly I acted. He trusted me with knowledge and I used it deliberately to wound him.' Cynthia appreciated her mother's loyalty, but knew that she was wrong.

'I think you are making a mistake in underselling his understanding, no matter what you think you have done.'

Jo's arrival interrupted their conversation and the continual flow of visitors after that gave them no chance to resume it. It was only when Lee, the male nurse, entered the room and firmly shooed everyone else out of the room that Cynthia had a moment to answer.

'I hope you are right, Mum. I will do whatever I can, but, in the end, it depends on him. I failed him and there is nothing that can change that.'

Jeanette squeezed her fingers gently and left the room, accepting Lee's insistence that his patient needed time to eat in peace and then rest.

Cynthia was pulling the telephone towards her by the cord when he returned.

'Whoa there, lady. Just what do you think you're up to?'

'I am going to make a phone call.'

'Not a problem. You just lay back and tell me the number and I'll put it on speaker for you. My instructions are to keep you from getting too ambitious for the moment.'

'You are a bully,' she accused.

'Yes,' he agreed. 'I get away with it too.'

'I want to talk to the florist.'

'Done,' he said, punching four digits on the touch pad. 'Gail, this is Lee from the eighth floor. I have the patient in eight twelve,' he paused, obviously interrupted. 'Yes, that's the one. She would like to speak to you.' He nodded, the futile gesture making Cynthia smile, and punched the speaker button.

'Gail,' she began. 'This is Cynthia Sheldon. I would like to speak to you about a delivery made to my room.'

'Yes, Cynthia. Is there a problem?'

'No. All the flowers are beautiful, particularly the rose. Do you have a record of who ordered it?'

226

'The order was phoned in Sunday night and they paid for it in cash this morning. I didn't speak to the man who ordered it and the woman who paid the cash didn't give her name.' Gail's voice was friendly, but professional.

'Then it was a man who ordered it.'

'Oh, most definitely. He certainly impressed my partner. Quite an authoritative voice, well educated, and he gave very precise instructions. Particularly that there was to be no card.'

That sounded more like her father than Drew. 'Was it a local call?' she asked.

'It came through the switchboard, so there was no way to tell.'

'M-m-m,' Cynthia said, speaking more to herself than to the telephone. 'The woman who paid the cash?'

'Young, well spoken, immaculately dressed, either one of the professions or senior executive level, I would guess. She confirmed his instructions and paid enough to cover a week's supply. If they discharge you before then we are to use the surplus to supply flowers to anyone we think needs them.'

That sounded like her father using one of the agency's staff as a messenger, yet he had been in the hospital himself and could have paid for it in person.

'Has that been any help?' Gail asked, accepting the silence as thought on

Cynthia's part.

'I think so,' Cynthia said. 'Thank you very much for your time. Once again, your flowers are beautiful.'

'Thank you. Goodbye.' The sharp click from the speaker signalled the disconnection.

'Finished?' Lee asked.

When she nodded, he replaced the telephone on the bedside table.

'You have the whole works lined up for you, Physio and masseur for a start. They will decide what comes after that, but you're booked into hydrotherapy later.'

God bless money, she thought, lying back in the bed. The room she occupied was barely recognisable as belonging to a hospital. They had disguised the essential equipment so tastefully that she had to look for it and Lee's constant attendance meant that he had few other duties. If she had to spend time in hospital, this was certainly the way to do it.

Contrary to her doctor's promise, the hospital did not discharge her until 48 hours later on the condition that an ambulance transport her to her home. Her mother had her old room ready and the appointments made for attending masseurs. Of all the flowers, she took only the rose, asking Lee to distribute the rest as he saw fit.

'I'll have to ask Gail to look after that,' he said. 'I am apparently coming with you.' He smiled at her surprise. 'Your mother has taken

228

a fancy to me. Do you think I will be safe with only you as a chaperone?'

'Do you want to be?'

'Your father looked far too ferocious for me to tackle,' he said, pretending to quake in fear. 'Then there is the mystery man with the authoritative voice. I think I'm safer if I just stick to nursing.'

'Do you want to come? I can stop it, if you want?'

'Don't go breaking my rice bowl, lady. They are paying me a bonus that has made my wife's eyes go glazed. I think she has already spent it at least twice.'

'All right then, but promise to tell me if you want out.'

'Unfortunately, it is only a week.'

A statement Lee may have regretted, once Jeanette Sheldon had taken charge in her own house. He quickly found Cynthia's room was his only refuge from her mother's barrage of instructions.

Like Lee, she was glad when the week was over and she could escape to her own apartment. She took her doctor's advice and did nothing about her other problems, mainly because she felt uncomfortable with her mother and Lee in constant attendance. Drew had already given her more chances than she deserved. She had to be very sure that she was ready before she tried again.

Jo was there to welcome her home. She

fussed about her for a while and then left to open the shop.

Cynthia sat for a while, enjoying the sun through the high studio windows and gradually building up her courage. The telephone call she was going to make would change her life. She had decided that it was safer to assume that her father had sent the single rose, although she had not quite found the nerve to ask him on his frequent telephone calls.

She found excuses three times before she managed to pick up the handset. She did not need to check the number. She had read it repeatedly during the last week. There were the usual noises, electronic beeps and burrs and the clack of a distant relay; then;

'Hello.'

Dulcie's voice was as clear as if she were only in the next room.

'Hello, Dulcie. This is Cynthia.'

The pleasure in Dulcie's response and her off-phone calls for Jack and Peter did much to offset the one name that was missing. Cynthia gave a report on her condition, explained that she was now home, sent her apologies to Peter for her vagueness on the morning that she left the homestead, and, finally, asked the question she had been dreading.

'Drew is not here, Cynthia. As soon as he finished the business with the police, he left.'

An abyss opened under Cynthia and she teetered on its edge.

'Do you know how I can contact him?'

'He didn't say,' the sympathy in Dulcie's voice told Cynthia more than she wanted to know. 'The legal implications are rather complex and it is going to take some months for the system to deal with them. I gathered from Drew's attitude that he would not be back until then. He's coming back to set things up. I really can't say any more.'

There was genuine regret in her voice. It made Cynthia assume that she knew more, but loyalty was compelling her to remain silent.

'He said that it was time that he found out if Drew Mitchell actually existed,' Dulcie said, offering what encouragement she could.

The reminder of her own words was a stab of pain that caught Cynthia unprepared and she drew a deep breath that was almost a sob. Dulcie must have heard, but she made no comment. They talked for a while and then ended the connection. Cynthia sat on the couch, as she had on another day, and let the sun pass slowly through the heavens while she fought to come to terms with this latest twist of the knife.

Either Dulcie knew where Drew was, and Drew had instructed her to say nothing, or Drew had gone off somewhere to be on his own while he shut her out of his life. There seemed little doubt either way that he considered the affair ended. She had failed the test of trust and must now begin her penance without even the hope of parole. She felt hollow inside, as if someone had carved out everything of worth and left only the outer shell.

That day passed, then the next. She returned to working in the shop with Jo, managing the accounts, planning as if she believed that a future existed, all the time hiding the emptiness inside. She deserved no better.

12

'Ms Cynthia Sheldon?'

She looked up from her desk in the back room of the store and saw the uniformed policeman flanking Jo.

'Yes . . . Sergeant,' she responded, rising to her feet as she identified his rank from the three chevrons on his sleeve.

The man before her was massive, built not unlike Jack, but with a physical hardness that went beyond mere strength.

'My name is Ted Hughes. This is not an official visit.'

That fact seemed important to him for some reason. It was as if he were deliberately distancing himself from the uniform that he wore. Cynthia was intrigued.

'Can we offer you a cup of tea or coffee?' Jo

asked, raising her eyebrows at Cynthia from out of his line of sight.

He turned back to her, his size making the movement seem almost ponderous.

'A cup of tea would be very nice, thank you.'

The exchange gave Cynthia the time that she needed. When he turned back, she was smiling.

'Please come in and sit down. Jo will be a few minutes fetching our drinks. Perhaps you would like to start by telling me how I may help you.' She indicated the chair beside the desk.

Her mother would have been proud of her imitation. It was pure Jeanette Sheldon.

The policeman thanked her and sat down gingerly. He appeared not to trust the chair and submitted it to his weight as if he expected it to crumble beneath him. When it withstood the test, he relaxed a little and lifted an old-fashioned briefcase to his knee. He busied himself with the strap that held it closed, fumbling with the buckle in a way that showed he was nervous. Cynthia sat quietly and waited.

'This is not an official visit,' he repeated, pulling out two items contained in ziplock bags of black plastic. One was quite large and looked like a foolscap-sized book. The other was quite small and barely bulked the plastic bag. He put them down carefully on the edge of her desk and then fished in the outer pocket of the briefcase to remove several sheets of A4 paper. They seemed to be some form of official report. He put these with the two parcels and then refastened the briefcase. It was a fascinating performance and her curiosity was now at a peak.

'I have decided to do it this way for several reasons,' he began. 'The most important is that my superiors would send me on extended stress leave if I went through official channels.'

He had taken so much time in his preparation and in commencing that Jo returned at that moment with their drinks. There was another pause while Jo distributed the cups, together with the sugar, milk and biscuits. He was in no hurry to start, sipping appreciatively at the tea before putting it down on the desk quite regretfully. Jo seated herself opposite him and this gave him the opportunity to delay even further by determining that she had the right to remain. When he was satisfied on this point, it was time for another sip of tea. Only then did he take up his story.

'Yes,' he said. 'They really wouldn't appreciate it. The senior sergeant, in charge of the Omeo police district, is not supposed to believe in ghosts.'

'You came up to Mitchell's Run the day that they flew me out,' Cynthia said, making the connection to the name Dulcie had used.

'Yes,' he confirmed. 'The body you

234

discovered in the mine was the business of the State Coroner. Drew called me up there before anything was disturbed and then assisted me in the investigation.'

'The investigation?'

'Yes. We now have proof that the body was that of Andrew Mitchell, who his family reported missing in 1886. Not only were there letters and possessions, tests carried out by the forensic pathologist sent by the Mortuary Services of the Department of Justice have confirmed the identity. My report, a copy of which you now have, closes the missing persons case and recommends that his possessions be turned over to his legal heir, Drew Mitchell.'

'Where do I come into it, Sergeant?'

'My report is accurate and truthful in everything that it says. It is, however, not complete. I have not included all the things that I found in the dead man's possession, nor the fact that you were present at the discovery. The two items on your desk do not appear on the official list. I authorised tests on both items and the only copies of the results are in the bags with them.'

'This all sounds very irregular, Sergeant, and you still have not explained why I come into the picture now.'

'One of the items, I believe to be yours. I am merely returning it. The other refers very specifically to you. The legal owner believes that you should have it and has relinquished all rights in your favour.' He picked up his cup, drained it and rose to his feet, picking up his briefcase. 'I had best be on my way. It's a long drive back to Omeo. Thank you for the tea. I hope to see you out my way some time so that I can repay the favour.' He turned abruptly and left the shop, leaving behind him a pool of silence.

Cynthia picked up the smaller bag and opened the ziplock fastener. Inside was a smaller bag of clear plastic labelled by the Mortuary Services. Inside the plastic bag was the pom-pom from her beanie. She turned the bag over to read the writing on the label. There were a series of identifying numbers and then a section for details. 'This item was found in the right pocket of the deceased. The bones of the right hand lay around it as if he was holding it when he died. Their dried state precluded the possibility of any person placing the object within their grasp after the discovery of the body. The item appears to be a woollen pom-pom, but its state of preservation is remarkable and it contains artificial fibres that were not in existence at the supposed time of death.'

Cynthia said nothing. She simply handed the package to Jo before turning her attention to the larger bag. This contained Andrew's journal. She recognised it immediately. It was the one she had seen with Andrew Mitchell's

236

skeletal remains. The note on the clear plastic inner bag read: 'This item was found with the deceased. It has been examined for any signs of tampering and is undoubtedly genuine.'

Jo read the note over her shoulder, having grown impatient.

'Curiouser and curiouser,' she said. 'What do you make of it?'

'I don't know,' Cynthia admitted. 'Let's see if the sergeant's report sheds any light on it.'

The report, in dry official language, described how the sergeant attended at the newly discovered mine and examined the body. It listed the possessions, which included 1137 ounces of gold, but did not mention the pom-pom or the journal. It concluded with a reference to the report of the forensic pathologist and the recommendation to close the missing person's case of Andrew Mitchell. It was brief, succinct, and explained nothing.

That left the journal.

Cynthia did not want to open it.

Whatever it said, it would not bring Drew back. She had now survived six weeks without him.

The first week, she had filled with 'if only she had done this' or 'if only she had done that'. The second week, she had called the private inquiry firm and they had discovered that Drew Mitchell had flown out to America two days before she called Dulcie, carrying all the cash he owned. There he had disappeared, perhaps going to friends, perhaps just buying a bus ticket, but leaving no trace. She thanked their representative and paid them off.

Since then, she lived the Alcoholics Anonymous creed of 'one day at a time' and she was slowly putting her life back together. The journal would not help that. It was best that it stayed unread. When it would no longer affect her, she would read it.

Jo was not amused. The police sergeant's visit had roused her curiosity and she wanted it satisfied, right now, but Cynthia held firm. She even took the journal out to her car and locked it in the boot out of temptation's way.

It stayed there all day. That night she carried it into her apartment. It could go with the rest of the file on Andrew Mitchell she had stored in the attic. One day, when all this was behind her, she would sit down and read it all as an ending. She felt the need for a cup of tea, so she placed the journal on the low coffee table temporarily. She would put it away afterwards. It was only by accident that she noticed the corner of a piece of paper protruding from between the pages and opened the journal a little to shift it into alignment. It looked so untidy. The edge of a drawing caught her eye and, just out of curiosity, she opened the journal a little more.

The torn page of a police notebook fell from her nerveless hand and the journal opened fully on the table as she stared at herself. It was a sketch of her face, executed in Indian ink. Below it, in his neat copperplate script, Andrew Mitchell had written *'The most beautiful thing I have ever seen.'* It destroyed whatever reservations she had against reading the journal.

Her need for a cup of tea now forgotten, she sat down on the couch and opened the journal at the first page. As they had suspected, Andrew completed the final sentence of the last journal as an opening. Not every entry was dated, and many of them were mundane. Andrew was suffering a plague of boils and he wondered if Surgeon Reynolds of the 24th was right when he put them down to poor food. A saddler had made a poor job of repairing the packsaddle and Andrew had made a sketch of the problem so he could discuss it with him some time in the future. For the moment, he had repaired it himself.

The first mention of the three thugs came on the tenth page. His description was quite scathing, He had crept close enough to their camp at night to listen to their talk and he knew as much about their purpose as they did. He did not appear to be worried. They were just a nuisance.

The abandonment of the high plains mine surprised her. Andrew had found a small pocket of gold the day before, but he was convinced there was nothing more. He was heading back to Mitchell's Run. There was a deadline coming up on the loan and he would have to risk the unstable ground of the overhang. Before he left, he raided the thug's camp, scattered their horses and stole the two kegs of blasting powder they were carrying. It was merely a warning, he did not harm any of the men.

He had dated the next entry, August 16th; she had become lost on August 15th. He was at the overhang above Mitchell's Run. He could even see the lights and was tempted to visit the homestead. She smiled as she read his words.

'I have obviously been away from women too long as I had a peculiarly vivid dream last night. Something called me from my sleep to rescue a young woman from the snow. It felt quite strange. We took refuge in the mine, but it was not the mine. Someone had extended it and it seemed lived in. I wish this work was as easy as dreams make it seem.

The young woman was very near death. She was almost unconscious when I reached her and needed bullying to make an effort. She had fallen in the creek and all her clothes were sodden and beginning to freeze. I got her out of them and dried her before using my body heat to warm her—the New England practice of 'bundling' would have been very enjoyable under other circumstances. Nathan Bradley told me how effective it had been in the Northern Army camps during the winters of their war, though I doubt his companions ever had so attractive a 'bundle' as I did. Unfortunately, I woke up about that time, but not before her features had been etched indelibly in my mind. I have done my best to capture them opposite. The one thing that really puzzles me is her body. My dream made it well formed, but quite athletic, more like the body of a Zulu maiden than a white woman. It is odd what images your mind captures. This was obviously triggered by the Zulu Induna's prophecy and that coloured my image of her.'

The journal returned to digging at the base of the overhang. It was quite dangerous, but he was winning enough gold to meet the loan deadline. He would continue for one more day at least. The bush greens he had found to supplement his diet had cleared up the last of the boils.

'August 18th. It was a good day yesterday. I struck a very rich pocket of gold in the seam and Goldilocks came back in my dreams. It was a continuation of the earlier dream. The cabin in the mine now seemed quite familiar. She woke and we ate together. Then we played chess, using the set I lost during the fight at Isandlwhana. She was very good, playing more like a man than a woman, though her strategy was more fixed than opportunistic. If she could learn to look at every opening rather than just concentrating on a single goal, she would do better. She would then be ready to grasp that ideal moment when it arrives, rather than looking back over her

241

shoulder at the one she missed. The dream ended when she went back to whatever world she sprang from and I was left alone in the mine that was obviously my home.'

There were two more entries about the progress of the digging and a total of the ounces won in the margin. Then a final entry:

'It would be nice to think that we grow smarter as we grow older, but there is no evidence of this in my case and it does not seem likely that I will live long enough to prove the contrary.

I should have killed those three men earlier. They had forfeited their right to live by hunting me. They are dead now, but I think they have killed both me and Mitchell's Run. They probably found me by accident, for I doubt that they had the skills to do it deliberately. I came out from the tunnel to find them fossicking through my camp. They all had rifles, but they panicked and fired wildly. I had hung Nathan Bradley's army revolver at the mouth of the tunnel and reached it while they were reloading. I ran back into the mine and the fools came after me. The light silhouetted them, allowing me to kill two of them and wound the third, before a ricochet took me in the side. I fell back as he scrambled out of sight. I do not know whether he meant to set off the blasting powder, but the explosion came almost immediately. The smoke was just clearing when the overhang slid down in front of the tunnel entrance trapping me in the tunnel. I can not reach the exit wound in my *back so I have made a thick pad and am leaning hard against the wall to stop the blood, but I can still feel it trickling.*

I have made another attempt to stop the bleeding, but I think it is too late. I am growing very cold and I have heard too many men complain of the cold as they died. The only thing that warms me is the memento Goldilocks left behind. I put on my coat against the cold and found it in my right pocket. I have it in my hand as I write. A pretty bauble made of wool.

I must have passed out for a while, or perhaps it was a waking dream, for I stood on the porch of Mitchell's Run. The moonlight was bright on the lake, bathing the valley beyond in silver. I do not know what made me turn, but I could see Goldilocks in the main bedroom. She was sitting in the bed and appeared to be waiting for someone.

Would that it had been for me.

The candle is dying and I do not have the strength to find another. I can barely see to write and the paler band on my wrist from the bandage that covered the last boil is all I can see of my left hand.

I wonder if there is anything in what the preachers say. I have sent so many ahead of me that I should be able to find acquaintances in either destination. Perhaps my lack of remorse will condemn me to limbo. It would be just.'

There was no more.

Cynthia sat there for a long time, the

243

journal closed on her knee. From the other side of the grave, Andrew had answered all her questions and left her with one last piece of advice. It was up to her how she used it.

The next few days were busy. The spate of Christmas parties always brought in the customers, most of them looking for that special outfit. It was the type of fashion at which Jo excelled. The days passed with hardly any time for lunch, let alone gossip and then late night shopping kept them both at it until closing time. A long hot shower and a cup of tea with her feet up were the important priorities at the end of each day and her mail accumulated on the hall table. By Sunday, it was threatening to spill onto the floor.

Cynthia picked it up and carried it to the lounge room coffee table. It was a formidable pile, but she reduced it rapidly by tossing all the junk mail into the bin unread. The remainder she sorted into business and personal then dealt with the business mail first. Four envelopes remained. One was from a friend, holidaying in the Greek Isles. The second was a chain letter, promising all sorts of good fortune if she would just send a copy to ten friends. That joined the junk mail. She recognised the writing on the third envelope. It was her mother's and the envelope contained an invitation they had already discussed. The writing on the fourth envelope was unfamiliar and the postmark obliterated.

She opened it and found a single sheet of bond paper with an embossed letterhead. It was from Dulcie Mitchell.

There was the usual greeting, an inquiry into her health, and that of her parents, before the important paragraph:

'The authorities have finally released Andrew's remains and it is our intention to inter him in the small family cemetery on the hill behind Mitchell's Run. The ceremony will only be for family members and for the very special people Andrew would have wanted to be there. There will be accommodation for everyone. Jack and Peter join me in asking that you come, if it is at all possible.'

There were another two paragraphs of general news, but no mention of Drew.

The date of the funeral was the following weekend, one that promised to be the busiest yet in the shop.

It took her almost a day to realise that she had no choice. She had to go. Drew would not miss the occasion and she could not miss the chance to speak to him face to face.

She rang Dulcie to confirm that she would be coming and the pleasure in the other woman's voice did much to dispel the cold knot of fear that grew with each passing minute. She had planned to drive up there on Saturday morning, but Dulcie advised her to wait for a few days before deciding on her transport arrangements.

'We have people coming from all directions. A lot of them will be flying in. It is more than probable that there will be a spare seat in one of the planes. I'll ring you back as soon as I can arrange something.'

There was no mention of Drew and Cynthia did not feel confident enough to raise the subject.

Two days later, Dulcie rang back and left a message on the answering machine. There was a helicopter lifting off from Essendon heliport at 10.00 a.m. Saturday and a seat had been reserved for her. She gave the address and a telephone number of the helicopter operator and suggested that Cynthia be there at least fifteen minutes before lift off.

Friday was a disastrous day: suppliers did not make deliveries on time; customers missed fitting appointments; and the temporary shop assistant sent by the agency turned up dressed in op shop clothes. It was nine at night before she managed to sort out the resulting shambles and she arrived home at her apartment to find an answering machine message from her father. He was home for the weekend and wanted her to ring him urgently. She was tempted to ignore the message. Her head ached, she had been on her feet most of the day, and she had not yet decided what was appropriate for a country funeral.

She delayed until after her shower and she was sitting on the couch with a hot drink.

'Hello, Dad. What are you doing home?'

'Just dropped in for a personal commitment. Can I see you early tomorrow?'

'I'm catching a helicopter at Essendon at ten o'clock in the morning.'

'Excellent. I have to go out there myself. I'll pick you up at 8.45. We can talk on the way out. Your mother tells me how busy you have been, so I'll let you get some rest. See you in the morning,' her father's voice ended in a sharp click as he hung up, leaving Cynthia staring at the telephone handset. Finally, she just shook her head. He would never change. Taking charge was a way of life for him.

An hour later she was still studying the contents of her wardrobe. The ubiquitous little black dress would be out of place in a family plot at Mitchell's Run and a tailored suit would be equally unsuitable. That left the option of a dark green dress or a blue-grey trouser suit. The dress was rather full and the blue-grey a little lighter than she really wanted. Dulcie had not really said how many there would be, or who, so she was left without guidance. Drew had already seen her in green, in burgundy, and in brown so the blue-grey seemed appropriate. It would be easier to manage getting in and out of the helicopter as well. That left accessories . . .

It was after midnight before she was packed and had laid out her clothes for the morning.

247

'Good morning, daughter. You look good enough to eat.'

'Thank you,' she replied, dipping slightly in a pretend curtsy.

He had to be lying. Sleep had been impossible. She had been up for hours, prowling her apartment like a caged animal. She had convinced herself that her appearance revealed her state to the world and had dared her mirror to confirm it. Her head felt as if it was full of cotton wool and her thoughts came slowly, if at all. The aspirin she had taken was obviously out of date and ineffective. If Drew was not at Mitchell's Run, she had no idea how she would survive the day. It made her appreciate her father's decision to pick her up in a chauffeured stretch limousine.

'I thought this would give us more freedom to talk,' he explained.

He looked much better than the last time she had seen him. There was a relaxed air about him, even dressed in a dark single-breasted suit. He actually looked rested.

He noted her glance. 'I have an assistant now. He and I will share the work in future. He is more than competent.'

'It's about time,' she said. 'Where did they find him?'

'They didn't say. They just sent him out to join me,' her father said with a smile, then paused briefly before continuing, almost as if he expected her to respond. 'Still, enough of him for the moment. I'm interested in you. What do you intend to do about Drew Mitchell. Your mother says that you have been moping around like a little girl who has lost her first pet.'

'It's a little more serious than that. I love him.'

'That hardly seems a cause for pain?'

The familiar quirk at the corner of his mouth reminded her of all the times he had stepped in and solved her problems when she was little. He had been her knight in shining armour until the aid agency had stolen him. The words came tumbling out and she explained the whole sorry mess she had made of things. He listened to it all and made all the right encouraging noises at exactly the right places.

'It sounds to me as if you know exactly what you want to do. All you have to do is manufacture the right opportunity. I would be surprised if you were not more than capable in that area.'

'That's where I am going today. They are burying Andrew Mitchell in the family cemetery at Mitchell's Run. I'm hoping that Drew Mitchell will be there.'

'Actually, it is where we are all going today. Your mother is meeting us at the airport. The man saved my daughter's life. It is only right that we pay our respects as a family.'

'Do the Mitchell family know you are coming?'

'Yes. We received a special invitation.'

She remembered the rapport that her father had established with Dulcie and Jack at Mitchell's Run after the landslide and believed him.

The Jeanette Sheldon who met them at the airport was a surprise. Cynthia could not remember her mother being so girlishly happy. She embraced the both of them as if they had been apart for months and almost blushed when Edward Sheldon whispered something in her ear, giving Cynthia a flashing look of pure happiness.

Her father introduced the other four passengers as they waited in the boarding lounge. The names meant nothing to her and the pilot interrupted immediately with a flight briefing so she had no chance to identify them. The pilot finished and there was a pause while he readied the aircraft. It gave her time to speak to her mother.

'You seem very happy,' she accused.

'I feel as if a nightmare has ended,' Jeanette Sheldon said, the glow in her eyes confirming her words. 'The new assistant that they sent Edward is marvellous. He and Edward will divide their time in Africa. Your father already trusts him implicitly.'

Cynthia was about to ask the name of this

paragon when the second pilot entered the lounge and announced that it was time to board the aircraft.

Her father was the last one to board, standing on the tarmac speaking earnestly to the second pilot and the office manager.

'Don't worry,' Jeanette announced to the others. 'I'm sure that my husband is giving exact instructions to the pilot on how to fly the aircraft. Fortunately, the pilots are sensible fellows and will ignore him completely.'

Cynthia was shocked at her mother's levity. It was a side of her that she had never seen before. Jeanette Sheldon was acting as if she had suddenly discovered the fountain of youth and drunk her fill. She envied her the happiness that could create such a transformation.

The helicopter flight was smooth and uneventful, except for her father passing written messages to the pilot. Helicopters are not ideal for conversation, so there was none, except through the headphones they wore. That was mainly the pilot's commentary and piped music. She did not mind, she was busy rehearsing what she would say to Drew when they met. Their meeting was critical. There would be no further chances for her. When the note of the blades above her head deepened and became separate, she was surprised to note that over an hour had passed.

'There is quite a bit of air traffic ahead,' the

pilot announced. 'I'm slowing down until they have all landed.'

There was an exchange between the pilot and her father, in which the pilot nodded quite deliberately and her father acknowledged with a nod of his own. Momentarily distracted from her own thoughts, she smiled at the familiar authority. Her father was undoubtedly paying for this flight and enjoying the exercise of his rights. He would never change in that respect.

The delay added about ten minutes to their flight time, making it just over ninety minutes; obviously the helicopter flew faster than the fixed wing aircraft Drew had borrowed. When they landed at Mitchell's Run, it was right next to the house. She could see a number of aircraft parked beside the bush strip below the dam. The high-winged monoplane Drew had flown was not amongst them.

Jack and Peter dealt with the luggage and helped the passengers down from the aircraft while Dulcie waited by the house. She greeted the others and then hugged Cynthia as if she had been away forever. There were tears in her eyes. The funeral was obviously very emotional for her.

'You are the last arrivals. We'll walk up the hill together and join the others.'

It was an easy walk, around the front of the house and along the bank of the dam to a set of steps carved in the hillside. At the top were two ancient gums that looked as if they had been there since the beginning of time. Clustered in their shade were a score of tombstones and amongst these stood a crowd of almost a hundred people.

She and Dulcie led the way. A sharp sense of urgency drove her now and Dulcie matched her pace, leaving the others to follow. As they came closer to the crowd, she searched for Drew, but could not see him. She looked again, pausing on each male face. He was not there!

Her shoulders slumped and her steps slowed, allowing the others to catch up. She had been so certain. Suddenly, her headache returned at full strength and tears welled in her eyes. The tiredness she had been holding at bay settled around her shoulders like a cloak and she could feel it soaking into her bones, turning them to chalk that would crumble at a touch.

She did not resist when her father took her arm and guided her to a place at the head of the open grave. Above the pit, a plain wooden coffin rested on trestles, the closed lid about waist high. She stepped forward and let her hand rest gently on its polished wood. It seemed impossible that so ordinary a thing could contain all that remained of Andrew Mitchell.

Another hand laid a single perfect red rose on the coffin—a match to the ones she had received each day in the hospital. She looked up to find Drew Mitchell standing beside her. The expression in his eyes answered all her questions.

'I believe you have met my new assistant,' her father observed. 'He thinks that your mother is the ideal person to make the wedding arrangements.'

It was obvious that the two men were already a formidable team. All the odd moments of the day suddenly fell into place. A pair of experts had manipulated her superbly, but it did not matter. She loved them both.

'Does Drew Mitchell really exist?' she asked.

'As long as he has your love.'

We hope you have enjoyed this Large Print book. Other Chivers Press or Thorndike Press Large Print books are available at your library or directly from the publishers.

For more information about current and forthcoming titles, please call or write, without obligation, to:

Chivers Large Print
published by BBC Audiobooks Ltd
St James House, The Square
Lower Bristol Road
Bath BA2 3BH
UK
email: bbcaudiobooks@bbc.co.uk
www.bbcaudiobooks.co.uk

OR

Thorndike Press
295 Kennedy Memorial Drive
Waterville
Maine 04901
USA
www.gale.com/thorndike
www.gale.com/wheeler

All our Large Print titles are designed for easy reading, and all our books are made to last.